The Summer Pact

SUNSHINE SERIES
BOOK THREE

LILLY MIRREN

Chapter One

The river water splashed gently against Beth Prince's paddle as her kayak pushed forward. It sliced through the water with ease, her arms straining with each pull. The rhythm was calming. Taking her kayak out was one of her favourite things to do. And there was a boat ramp close to her flat, which made it easy to get out onto the Brisbane River whenever she liked.

The sun was on its way towards the horizon, and even though it was five o'clock in the evening, she still had another hour or more of daylight, since November days were long and only getting longer as summer approached. She loved this time of year. The air was warm on her bare shoulders, the water splashed quietly with each dip of the oar, and behind her was the hum and buzz of the city.

She missed Sunshine and her family. She liked living in Brisbane, but if her job wasn't located there, she would've stayed on Bribie Island. That was home to her. She'd adapted to city life, paddling on the muddy river instead of in the bay with the sea turtles and dolphins cruising by and poking their heads up to watch her with curiosity. But she couldn't help pining for the coastal life she'd left behind.

Still, there were no jobs in Sunshine. She'd had to take what she could find. And she'd been drawn to Brisbane by the prospect of seeing her boyfriend, Brad, more often. Even though he worked for the mines and was gone most of the time, when he was back, he stayed in his flat in Toowong. She'd rented one in the same building so they could be close to one another.

They'd dated for six months so far. The time had flown by, so it felt like one month. In that time, he'd only been back for one week out of each of those six months. But when he was home, they went out to restaurants, danced at the clubs in the city, hiked, swam and kayaked together. It was a fun relationship, one she had enjoyed so far. But she wasn't entirely sure where it was headed. He'd been back at the mines for the past two weeks and had only called her once.

Her kayak clunked into the end of the dock. She grabbed hold of it, then clambered out. She pulled the kayak up onto the dock, and it scraped across the timber. Then she set it on the trolley she'd used to bring it down to the river and wheeled it back up to the road.

The street was busy—cars bumper-to-bumper on their way home from the office. She walked to the crossing and waited for the lights to change, then wheeled the kayak across the street and into her building. It wouldn't fit in the lift, so she stowed it in the underground parking garage inside the lockable storage area in front of her car.

Upstairs in her flat, she took a shower. By the time she was dressed in a tank top and shorts, her wet hair still dripping onto her shoulders, she was starving. It'd been a long day at the office, and she was still reeling from several stressful meetings they'd had. She was on the multimedia team, responsible for several branding projects at a large communications consulting company. But client billings were down, and everyone was scrambling to find more billable hours before the end of the month.

She decided on a creamy pasta with prawns and spinach for dinner. While she was cooking, she flicked on the television so she could watch the news. But as soon as she did, her phone rang. She turned off the TV and the stove and hurried to answer it. It was Brad. He often called at this time, but she wasn't usually home. She'd finished work early today so she could kayak and clear her head.

"Hey," she said as she jumped onto the couch and criss-crossed her legs.

"Hey, baby," he replied. "I didn't think I'd catch you."

"I came home early. Work was crazy."

"Sorry to hear that. What happened?"

"They're stressed about finances. We're not billing enough. I'm worried they're going to do layoffs, and I haven't been there long. It could end up being a last-in, first-out type of situation."

"They know you're good at what you do. I don't think you have anything to worry about." He cleared his throat. "Listen, I'm not going to make it back to Brisbane next week."

"Oh? What's going on?"

"I've got to get a break—have some downtime. You know? I'm tired. Going back and forth is wearing me out."

"Okay, I can understand that. But I'll miss you." She couldn't help feeling disappointed. He'd visited her once per month lately rather than every couple of weeks the way he'd done early in their relationship. But even when he was there, he was absent-minded. Always on his phone, laughing at someone's text messages, watching videos. He hadn't given her much attention the last time he was home, complaining of a sore throat, which confined him to his flat for most of the week. Was something going on that he wasn't sharing with her?

"I know, babe. But the thing is, I think we're probably on different paths. You know what I mean?"

She frowned. "Not exactly... I thought we both wanted the same thing."

"You're busy with work in Brisbane, and I'm up north most of the time. We don't see each other much. I think it'd be better for both of us if we opened ourselves up to other experiences."

"What does that mean? Other experiences?"

"Other people, activities, events... that kind of thing."

Her heart raced, and anxiety travelled up her spine. Was he saying what she thought he was saying?

"Do you mean you want to see other people?"

"We can still hang out when I'm in Brisbane," he replied.

She shook her head slowly. How could she have been so blind? She wanted to be with someone who was looking for marriage, settling down, a family. It wasn't something she'd thought a lot about in the past, but now that she was drawing closer to thirty, she was ready to put down some roots. She'd thought he was on the same page as her. He'd seemed very content in their relationship for the first few months. He'd been the one to push for a more serious connection between the two of them. And now he was pulling away. Her heart squeezed.

"I don't want that. I don't want to see other people."

"Sorry, babe. This isn't working for me. You know how I am—I need to have interactions, and we don't see each other much."

"Then move back to Brisbane. Find a job here."

"I love my job," he replied with irritation in his voice. "You can't ask me to do that."

She didn't respond. He clearly wanted to break up with her. And she wasn't going to stop him, even though it hurt her to stay quiet.

After she hung up the phone, she leaned against the bench for several long minutes with a hard lump forming in her throat. Then she shook it off and went back to cooking dinner. She set some jazz music to play and tried her best to relax. She was upset about the breakup, but not upset enough to cry. And that should really be a sign to her that it was the right thing to do. She wouldn't have taken the action herself, since she liked Brad and enjoyed spending time with him. But if he really was the one for her, wouldn't she at least shed a few tears over losing him?

Chapter Two

The next day, she decided to skip the train and walked to work. She set out an hour earlier than usual and walked down the bike path towards the city. The river glinted under the morning sunlight. Ferries chugged by. Bicycles flew past. The sun was warm on her head. It was a bright new day, and she already felt a little better than she had the previous evening.

So, Brad didn't want to keep seeing her. Or, in his words, he also wanted to see other people. Something she couldn't stomach. She had no desire to be one of many dates on his contact list. She was looking for something more special than that. But was she being unrealistic? Times had changed, as her mother constantly reminded her. Were there still people falling head over heels in love and committing their lives to one another? Or was she destined to date a series of Brads well into her thirties, and then desperately undertake a round of IVF to have children? She'd never been one to dream of being a mother. It was simply something that was always there, in the background. Something she'd taken for granted.

As one of four children, she was accustomed to having a large, happy, loud family. But lately, there were a few things that had shaken up her worldview. The first was her parents' divorce. As much as she told them she supported their choices and wasn't angry with them for breaking up the family—she was an adult after all, and thirty was not far off—it had hurt her, perhaps more deeply than she'd realised at first. If they couldn't make it work, could anyone?

Her parents seemed happy. They'd spent decades together, raised a family together. They'd been good parents. She could see, of course, how her father had neglected her mother. He was a good man, but wasn't particularly adept at expressing how he felt, and he had a tendency to be selfish. Still, she could see the best in him. She was his only daughter, and he'd doted on her over the years.

Their separation and divorce had knocked the wind from her lungs. She had to admit that it probably impacted the way she viewed romance and relationships—was anything lasting? What was she looking for? Did she want someone different to her father, someone who wasn't so absorbed in his career? She'd thought Brad might be that man.

They were very different to one another. She was a graphic designer. He drove large trucks for a living. To be honest, she wasn't exactly sure what he did, but it involved moving dirt around. Perhaps she should've asked more questions, but whatever he did, it didn't seem as though he was particularly career focused. He'd appeared to be the kind of man who might put aside aspirations if they interfered with his family relationships. And yet now he had broken up with her because of his job. It seemed like an excuse rather than a reason.

Obviously, it wasn't his job that was the problem. If he'd loved her, he would've made it work. It was a hard thing to face, but clearly he *didn't* love her. And if she was being honest, she couldn't say she loved him either. She'd hoped one day it might come to that. But perhaps she should've known by now, six months into the relationship, whether it would go anywhere further. Jemma, her best friend, certainly thought so. She'd told her many times over the months that when she found the right man, she'd know. Jemma had fallen in love with her husband in the span of about three dates. But how many people had that kind of luck?

She needed to speak to Jemma. But Jemma was a marine biologist who lived on Bribie Island in Beth's hometown. And she'd be at work, probably with a snorkel in her mouth, submerged beneath the ocean's surface. She wouldn't be able to talk. So, Beth would simply have to wait until the end of the workday to give her friend a call.

* * *

The office was particularly tense when Beth got settled in front of her computer. She glanced around, noticing how many people were on the phone, voices raised. Her boss's desk was empty, which wasn't unusual, given how many meetings she had on a daily basis. But the graphic design team were all at their respective places, working hard. They were some of the few people in the office who didn't have client meetings and didn't have to find their own client accounts. Their boss did all of the networking on their behalf. Their jobs were more technical than the rest of the company, who were mostly involved in writing reports or negotiating with stakeholders on behalf of their clients.

Anne clacked across the polished concrete floors with a takeaway coffee cup in hand. As usual, her hair was perfectly shiny as it fell in soft waves down her back. Her short skirt showed off thin legs above a pair of impossibly high heels. She smiled with a pout of red lipstick.

"Good morning. You're in bright and early this morning."

Beth sighed. "I walked. Thought it might help me relax."

"What's going on?" Anne half-sat on the edge of Beth's cubicle.

"Brad broke up with me." She didn't much want to talk about it, but she might as well spread the word. It was bound to be office gossip for several days. She should get it over with as soon as possible.

"I'm so sorry to hear that. What happened?"

"He didn't say, not really. But I think the distance didn't help."

"Of course it didn't. You poor thing. We'll grab some lunch later and you can tell me all about it. There's a staff meeting first thing, by the way. Just a heads-up—the big boss doesn't look happy."

Anne was the CEO's personal assistant, and she knew everything that was going on in the company — she rarely gave details, just vague warnings and innuendo. She could be fired for saying more.

"Tread lightly. That's all I'm saying."

"Thanks for the warning. Hey, listen. I mocked up a design for the Howard brand."

"Oh, let me see," Anne said. "Mark Howard is a personal friend of the boss's, so he's anxious to make sure he gets the best service we can offer. He keeps asking me about it, but I haven't had anything to report yet."

Beth pulled up the files she'd worked on. The brand was subtle, in subdued colours. It was for a financial advisory firm and needed to be professional, understated and classic. That was the brief.

"Wow, Beth, you've outdone yourself again. That's perfect. He's going to love it."

"I'm glad you think so." Beth smiled. "And I brought you some of those cookies you love. I baked some late last night." She pulled a baggie filled with large chocolate chip cookies out of her purse and handed it over to a wide-eyed Anne.

"Ooooh, thank you. This is going to be perfect with my morning coffee."

"You're welcome. I needed a sugar fix last night, and my sugar-free hot chocolate just wasn't going to do the job." Beth laughed. "Breaking up requires real sugar."

"Yes, it does. I'm sorry about Brad. Let me know if there's anything I can do to help."

"You being here helps," Beth said. "Thanks."

Ten minutes later, it was time for Beth to attend the staff meeting. She remembered what Anne had said and chose to sit near the back of the space. They met in an open area beside the kitchen where there were various cushions to sit on, but most of them stood. Beth chose a wall to lean against, with the rest of the graphic design team. They were all particularly moody today and barely said a word to one another. Beth spotted Anne standing beside her boss, Ken Armitage. He wore an open-collared shirt with a pair of expensive slacks. He always looked as though he'd stepped out of the pages of *GQ Magazine*.

He clapped his hands together and gave his signature blazingly white smile to the group. "Good morning, people. Glad to see you're all here on time and in fine spirits."

There were murmurs of agreement all around. It was always a competition to see who could make the boss happiest. Beth hated the competitiveness of it, the sucking up. She kept out of it as much as possible. Thankfully, their team didn't have much interaction with Armitage on a daily basis. He wasn't particularly interested in graphics, being a comms guy himself.

He made a few announcements. There was a birthday cake for one of the admin staff. Then finally, Armitage cleared his throat and raised his hands for silence.

"I have one final announcement, and unfortunately, it's a hard one to make. As you know, our billable hours have been low and getting lower in recent months. This is one of the most difficult aspects of the industry we work in—the ups and downs are a part of life for us. And as such, we're going to have some layoffs today that will be particularly difficult for many of you."

As he went through the details, Beth froze. He said "graphics team." Did he mean the whole team? Was he referring to layoffs, or just a reorganisation? He'd mentioned both. Which was her team going to be part of? Had she just lost her job?

After the meeting was over, everyone drifted away except her own team. They all stood huddled together, stunned. Then they meandered back to their desks. The general consensus was that they were confused, but they thought perhaps they had all been let go. When Beth got to her desk, this was confirmed by an email in her inbox with instructions. She gaped silently at it for several minutes, then began walking through the steps.

1. Set up out-of-office email auto responder
   2. Remove personal files from computer
   3. Clear out desk
   4. Report to supervisor and hand over in-progress work product
   5. Notify HR and return office access card
   6. Return computer to IT Support
   7. Leave the office

It took her two hours to complete the tasks, but then she was done. She said goodbye to Anne, who was mortified but couldn't say so, since the boss was only metres away on a phone call. He gestured wildly and laughed loudly. Beth waved at Anne, who slumped down behind her desk with a sympathetic look on her face.

Then she walked home. She felt numb. First, Brad had broken up with her. Now she'd lost her job. A job she was good at. A job she'd felt confident in until the past few days. What would she do? Would she find something else?

Suddenly, she didn't want to stay in the city. It was hot, lonely and isolating here. She had friends, but most of them were in Sunshine, along with her family. She felt rejected and insecure, and she needed to go where she knew she was loved and welcome. She wanted to go home.

Chapter Three

Gwen Prince tiptoed down the hall, past her guest room where Beth was soundly sleeping, and then slipped into her shoes in the kitchen. She used the stainless-steel fridge door as a mirror to check her makeup, then foraged around in the fridge for a small tub of non-fat strawberry yoghurt. If she was still hungry, she'd eat something more at the restaurant when she got to work.

She stood at the bench to eat her yoghurt while perusing the news on her iPad. Then she hurried to the hall mirror to re-check her hair. Her bob had grown out a little but was only just brushing against her shoulders. She had natural waves and had supplemented them with some hot rollers the day before, which gave her hair a beachy look. Her ex-husband had preferred her hair straight, so she'd spent many years straightening it. But now that she was no longer married to him, she'd embraced the curls and enjoyed the freedom from spending so much time in front of a mirror.

It was November, and Aurora, her boutique inn and bistro, had been open for six weeks. Aurora had already sparked buzz across the island, and the bookings had been rolling in a little at a time, growing in momentum as the weeks passed. She was grateful they'd opened in time for the peak summer season and was looking forward to seeing how they fared over Christmas.

Beth padded out of her bedroom wearing a pair of silk pink pyjamas. She yawned and rubbed her eyes.

"Sorry, honey. Did I wake you? I tried to be quiet," Gwen said as she turned on the kettle.

"It's okay. I'm used to waking up early. I can't really sleep late these days."

"How are you feeling?"

"I'm okay." She sat on a bar stool at the counter.

"Tea?" Gwen asked.

"Yes, please."

"Have you heard from Brad?"

Beth shook her head. "I don't think I will."

"It's his loss. He clearly doesn't know how much he's going to miss you."

Beth smiled. "Such a mum thing to say."

"Well, it's true. I'd miss you so much if I didn't get to have you in my life anymore."

Beth laughed. "Glad to hear it."

"I'm sorry, but I have to go to work. I'd love to call in sick, but I'm the boss. What will you do today?"

Beth sighed. "I guess I'll just hang around here. Maybe take a walk on the beach."

"That sounds nice. There's a lovely walk around the headland."

"I know, Mum. I've lived here almost my entire life."

"Of course you have," Gwen replied in a singsong voice as she poured hot water into two mugs. Hers was a travel mug. She left the tea bag and added milk. Then her phone rang.

"Hello, this is Gwen speaking."

"Gwen, it's Mallory." The manager at the inn called her

frequently to get her input and advice. Gwen hoped it was only growing pains and that she'd learned to make decisions independently before too much longer. Gwen spent half her time on the phone when she wasn't at the inn herself.

"Good morning, Mallory. I hope everything went okay. Did the overnight manager report anything of concern?" They'd had a few broken items in need of repair, and things that'd been installed incorrectly such as the heating in one of the bathrooms. But they were gradually working through the list.

"There's been an mishap. Could you please come to the inn as soon as possible? One of our guests is dead."

* * *

When Gwen arrived at the inn, the police were already there. Their vehicle and an ambulance were parked outside in the curved driveway, lights flashing. Gwen hurriedly parked her Mercedes coupe in the reserved parking space with her name on it, then rushed in through the side door, heart hammering against her ribcage. She found the manager, paramedics and police on the second level inside one of the bedrooms.

It was quiet in the room. There was no bustle of activity. There was a man lying prone on the bed in a pair of boxer shorts. A woman stood against the wall, wearing a white bathrobe cinched around a narrow waist. The couple looked to be around Gwen's age.

Gwen approached Mallory and whispered a greeting. Mallory gave her a stricken look.

"He died a little while ago. The wife called to let us know and I called the ambulance. I didn't know what else to do. Is there anything I should be doing?" She wrung her hands together, her brown eyes flitting between Gwen's face and the man on the bed.

Gwen patted her on the shoulder. "You did the right thing, Mallory. Good work. The police and paramedics can handle it from here. Our job is to take care of his wife, who is our guest. Do you know their names?"

"Marco and Francesca Silver," Mallory replied. "They were supposed to stay all week."

Six weeks into the opening of her new inn and bistro, and someone had already died on site. That wasn't a good start. What would the press say about it? She immediately felt guilty for that thought. Her focus should be on the stricken wife, not the marketing for her inn. She joined the wife on the other side of the room and murmured in a quiet tone.

"Hello, Francesca. My name is Gwen, and I own the inn. I'm so sorry for your loss. Is there anything we can do to help you right now? Would you like me to call someone for you? Get you a cup of tea? Anything at all?"

Francesca turned to face her. She was an attractive woman with dyed brown hair that was piled on top of her head in a messy bun. Her wide brown eyes were glassy but dry. She held a perfectly manicured hand to her mouth, the red nails accentuating her pale skin.

"Thank you so much. You're very thoughtful. I would love a cup of tea. I'd like to call my daughter in Italy and I can't seem to locate my mobile." Her accent was soft and lilting, her voice deep.

"I would be more than happy to help you with that."

"Thank you."

"Would you like to make the call? Maybe in our dining room or the sitting room? I can shut the doors and give you privacy. Not many people are up yet."

Francesca glanced back at her husband's body, her face turning stony. "Thank you. I think I will." She faced the paramedics. "Please let me know when you are leaving so that I may say goodbye."

She sobbed once but stopped there. The paramedics nodded in agreement. Francesca followed Gwen to the sitting room downstairs. Gwen flagged down one of the staff and asked them to bring tea and a breakfast muffin for Francesca. Then they went to her office and shut the door to make the phone call.

Francesca had the phone on speaker. The call was as awful as Gwen imagined it would be. The daughter was hysterical and difficult to understand through her tears. Francesca seemed determined to hold herself together, and Gwen was impressed by her stoicism. Some people didn't like to confront their emotions head-on. But Gwen felt tears well in her own eyes at the daughter's grief.

She stayed behind in the office to give the daughter details on how to reach the inn. When she came out of her office, she saw Francesca kissing her dead husband goodbye. Then she pulled the sheet back over his head and watched the paramedics wheel him out to the ambulance, hugging herself with both arms. Gwen walked over to stand beside her in silence, **her heart aching.**

Chapter Four

The next day, Beth went for another walk on the beach. The one the day before had ended with her being soaked by a sudden summer downpour. But today was clear, without a cloud in the sky. The birds were in fine form, singing at the tops of their lungs. Everything looked fresh and newly washed. She skipped out of the apartment complex and onto the footpath that wound its way through the dunes to the beach.

It was good to be back in Sunshine. She didn't miss the city one little bit. It felt like a huge weight had been lifted from her shoulders and she could breathe again. She hadn't realised how constricted and burdened living alone in a flat in a busy neighbourhood so far from home had made her feel. And now that she was back on the island, a sense of peace had settled over her. She missed Brad, less today than yesterday, so maybe the loss would fade over time.

As she plunged through the soft, dry sand, toes pointing downwards to give her leverage, she thought about the coming New Year and her impending birthday. She would be twenty-eight years old, and she was once again single. Still not married. Still no children. Starting over from scratch with no potential relationship in sight. How long would it be until she met someone? And from there, how much longer until they were ready to commit? What if he bailed on her after six months or a year, and she had to begin looking for Mr Right all over again?

This could go on indefinitely. The thought made her stomach clench. She'd been anxious about any number of other things—paying bills, choosing the right career, getting ahead in her career, not saying the wrong thing at parties, losing friends over silly miscommunications, flying. There were plenty of things in the world to stoke a panic attack. But romance and family had never been one of them for her. Now, all of a sudden, she felt differently. It'd been so much easier when she was younger.

After a few minutes, she broke into a jog. Her bare feet slapped against the damp sand with each step. The waves were small and scurried up the beach towards her, splashing around her feet and ankles before retreating again. Her thoughts returned to the boy she'd met fifteen years ago, her very first crush. It'd been an intense night. They'd met on New Year's Eve and spent the entire night getting to know one another. They'd watched the sun rise together on a brand-new decade. It'd been an incredible and life-altering experience for her.

One night. It was nothing, really, but it was the best night of her life. A night she never forgot. She wrote his name all over her high school binder. There'd been a big heart scrawled in red on the front, with his initials plus her initials in the centre. The word *forever* looped beneath it, with kisses and hugs all around it.

Everyone in her class at school had known about the mystery guy, but they didn't know any details. She kept that to herself. Only his name was public domain. Damien, from Dee Why. She didn't even know his last name. She hadn't thought to ask it. She'd tried to find him a couple of times over the years, but Damien from Dee Why didn't exist. Not online or in telephone directories, anyway. Was he real? She'd seen him, spoken to him, touched him. But then he'd vanished, and she'd never seen or heard from him again. She'd hoped every summer afterwards that his family might return to Sunshine for a holiday, but they never had. At least, she hadn't seen him if they did.

He was like no other boy she'd ever met before. He was handsome in a way that made her heart skip a beat every time she looked into his golden-brown eyes. But he was also earnest, fun and with no self-consciousness. At the time, she was accustomed to boys who were shy, withdrawn or disinterested in conversations with girls. They were thirteen, after all, and thirteen-year-old boys weren't exactly thrilling for a thirteen-year-old girl. Even when they had dance class in PE, she'd recoiled from holding hands with the sweaty, stinky boys she'd attended school with.

But Damien was different. A year older than her, he had an air of maturity and confidence while also being humble, kind and funny. In short, he was perfect. At least, that was how she remembered him. Maybe she had rose-coloured glasses about the whole situation. It was a long time ago. Perhaps her memories had altered reality, and he was actually someone entirely different to who she'd crafted him to be in her mind. But she didn't think so. She'd been in love with him from the moment she met him, but in a cruel twist of fate, his family left to return to the Sydney suburb where he lived the very next day.

Their parting words echoed in her mind.

"If we're both single fifteen years from now, we should meet again here on New Year's Eve," she'd said, pushing her long ponytail back over her shoulder.

He'd smiled at that. "And get married."

"Married?"

"Yeah, if we're both single."

She'd liked the sound of that. "Okay, it's a deal. We'll meet here in fifteen years and get married."

He held out his hand to her, and she shook it. "Deal. See ya then."

And that was that. He'd walked away with a wave and a grin, one dimple playing in his cheek as he glanced back at her. She'd felt her heart break into pieces as his family car drove away, the glow of morning sunshine still weak against the semi-darkness of dawn.

* * *

Back at the flat, she took a quick shower and got changed into another pair of yoga pants and a crop top. She was unemployed. Why not wear yoga pants everywhere? It was comfortable, and she couldn't be bothered dressing up. What would be the point?

She made herself a cappuccino with her mother's fancy new espresso machine. Mum was at the inn, she'd called Beth on her mobile a few minutes earlier. Beth felt bad for her—one of the guests had died the previous day, even though they'd only been open for a couple of months, and her mother was very stressed out about it. She'd tried to play it down, but Beth knew her better than anyone and could tell how much she was worried about the guest's wife and the whole situation, including what it might mean for the inn.

While Beth ate a bowl of muesli, she turned the television on to watch the daily morning show. She loved the show, but she only ever watched it when she was on holiday, since it didn't air until after she was already at work during the week. It felt luxurious to be able to sit on the couch with her bowl of cereal in hand, watching the news and fun personal interest segments.

Just then, the story of the man dying at her mother's inn came on. She sat up straight and stopped chewing to listen. It covered the details of the case briefly, and then it was over and they'd moved on. They hadn't mentioned the inn by name, they showed a video shot of it in the background as the reporter spoke. There was no way to identify the place by that, though. She leaned back on the couch with a sigh of relief. Mum should be happy about that.

After breakfast, she scanned the employment ads and sent in a few applications for jobs in the Brisbane area. There wasn't much around, but she was confident she'd find something. It might take longer than she'd hoped, though. She'd have to make some calls and reach out to her contacts. Networking was the best way to get a position—she'd never landed an interview from an online advertisement before, but there was no harm in trying.

Then, she worked on breaking her apartment lease and was grateful to discover that the lease would end naturally within a few weeks. So she called the management to let them know she wouldn't be renewing, then looked for a removal company to take her things to storage until she located somewhere else to lease.

By morning teatime, she was ready to get out of the flat. She grabbed her purse and headed for the door. But when she stepped outside, she saw a small, scruffy dog. It had probably been white at some point in its life, but now it was dirt-coloured, with matted hair in desperate need of a trim. It looked up at her with mournful eyes but didn't attempt to get out of her way.

"What are you doing here?" she asked, glancing around the hallway.

There was no one to be seen. She bent to pat the dog, and it responded with a gentle wag of the tail. It seemed tired. Perhaps it was hungry as well. Surely it belonged to someone in the building.

She knocked on every door on that level, but most people weren't home, and the ones who were didn't know anything about a dog, and the creature kept following her around. Finally, she picked it up and carried it inside. She'd have to take it to the vet to see if it had a microchip with the owner's details registered, but for now it needed a bath.

Chapter Five

Two days later, Francesca Silver still hadn't checked out, and Gwen was beginning to wonder if she should say something. Perhaps the poor woman thought she was required to finish her stay, but Gwen would make sure she knew she was free to go. She couldn't imagine what Francesca was going through, but the woman had spent the past three days keeping very much to herself. When she emerged from her room, she wore a silk scarf over her hair and oversized sunglasses.

Gwen was at the reception counter when Francesca appeared. She stopped in the centre of the reception area and scanned the room as though looking for something. Gwen hurried to meet her.

"Hello, Francesca. How are you today? Is there anything I can get for you?"

"Oh, hi, Gwen. You can call me Fran. I was wondering if someone could give me a recommendation for lunch today. I thought I might venture out. Is there somewhere good to eat?"

"What are you in the mood for?"

"Seafood, I think. I'm at the beach. When I'm near the ocean, I always love to eat seafood."

Gwen pondered for a moment. "I can recommend Snappers. The name sounds a little like a fish-and-chip shop, but it's actually a very classy seafood place with the most delicious Morton Bay Bugs."

"That would be fine," Fran replied.

"Fran, do you mind if I ask...." Gwen hesitated, looking for the right words. "How are you going with everything?"

"I'm holding up the best that I can."

"If you need to leave the inn, I'm very happy to give you a refund. You don't have to stay if there's somewhere else you have to go, you know, for funeral arrangements and so on."

Fran shook her head. "I've requested an autopsy. I want to find out what killed my husband. I've been told it will take a while. And besides, I know he'd want to be buried in Italy. I want to give people time to book a flight and accommodations. He'll be cremated after the autopsy, and then we can take our time to put together a memorial service."

"Oh, that's a good idea."

"There's really nowhere else for me to go right now. I don't want to go home, and my family is scattered around the world."

"You're very welcome here. Stay as long as you need. I can clear any other bookings if you'd prefer to remain here longer. It's entirely up to you. We're here to support you in any way we can."

"Thank you. I appreciate that. I knew this was a wonderful establishment from the moment we walked through the door. It has that feel about it. I can tell, you see."

Gwen smiled. "I'm glad to hear it. What do you do for a living?"

"I worked in hospitality for many years, when I wasn't raising my children."

"Hospitality?"

"Hotels, mostly. I worked all over the world, which is why my children live in different places now. They live where they spent their formative years. Marco and I both worked in hotels and resorts. He was a hotel manager and I was a concierge, and I filled various other roles at different times."

Gwen had a moment of clarity. "Are you working anywhere now?"

"No, I haven't worked in five years. Marco wanted to retire and travel, so that's what we've been doing. We rented a place up north, but we hardly stay there. We've never bought a home since we moved so often, and now that Marco is gone..." She stifled a sob with her fist. "I don't really know what to do with myself. Should I go back to our rental in Hervey Bay? It'll be so lonely. I could travel to stay with one of the kids, but they have their own lives, and besides, I want to stay here in Australia. This is my home now. I've been gone from Italy too long." She smiled sadly. "So you see, that's why I've stayed. And perhaps I should've checked out and gone home, but all that waits for me there are a few dead plants and an empty house."

Gwen's mind raced. She couldn't ask Fran to work for her, could she? Her husband had died three days ago. It was too soon. But maybe she would like the distraction, and Gwen desperately needed a new concierge. One of their staff had quit the previous day and left her in the lurch. She wanted someone with experience, but that was hard to find in Sunshine.

"I have a proposal for you, and you can certainly turn me down. There's no pressure. I know this is a very difficult time for you, but would you consider working here? I have an opening for a concierge, and I think you would be a perfect fit. What do you say?"

Fran's eyes filled with tears. She squeezed her lips together for a moment, then smiled through the tears. "Really? I would love that. It would be just what I need."

Chapter Six

Joanna Gilston had entered a new phase of life. She felt as though she'd woken up after a long, restless sleep. The past year had brought so much change, she had quite a different outlook than previously. She was positive. Happy, even. She wasn't afraid to leave the house any longer. Her agoraphobia was gone. There were times when she felt the anxiety creeping back, but mostly she was quite comfortable going outside into wide-open spaces, and the freedom was intoxicating. At sixty-one years of age, she felt younger than she had in a decade.

She fixed her grey hair in the mirror, combing it back until it lay smooth and sleek against her scalp. Then, with a grin, she trounced out to the kitchen. She was excited about the day ahead of her. Emily was coming over. She hadn't seen Emily in weeks. Today they were preparing the food for tomorrow's Potluck Brunch. They were focusing on American-style food this month, Southern or soul food, and she was thrilled. It was one of her favourite styles of cuisine, although she always said that. She loved food. No matter where it was from.

Their cookbook sales continued to rise, and the publisher was effusive about the results of their marketing. They'd gotten Joanna and her friends to do a series of very silly TikTok videos, much to their dismay. Joanna had felt extremely awkward and out of touch with the younger audience. But apparently the videos had resonated with the market and had boosted sales substantially across the world. She shook her head as she thought about it. It didn't make much sense to her, but she was grateful for it.

There was a knock at the door, and with a grin, Joanna hurried to answer it. She swung the door open. Emily stood there with a bottle of wine in her hands.

"You're here!" Joanna exclaimed, embracing Emily. "I'm so glad. Come on in."

Emily set the wine on the bench. "I'm so glad I didn't have to drive up from Brisbane. The traffic gets worse by the month."

"You're staying with Wanda for the holidays? How's it going with your sister? Is she doing okay?"

"Yes, we're all living on top of one another. She's coping well. She's very resilient. I never would've thought that when we were young, since she complained a lot at the time. But having to deal with cancer seems to have brought out a remarkable inner strength. I'm always telling her she's the strongest person I know."

"Left alone with two small children and then dealing with cancer. It's a lot for anyone to tackle. I don't know how she manages, to be honest."

Emily washed her hands at the sink. "She doesn't have a choice. I guess that's all there is to it."

Joanna hesitated. She wanted to frame her question in a gentle way, but she was curious and had been for a long time. "Did Brian leave before or after her diagnosis?"

Emily wiped her hands dry. "He left right after."

"Wow. I'm so sorry."

"I know. It was shocking to me at the time, but according to her doctor, it happens a lot."

"How awful."

"She was devastated."

"Of course she was."

"He's the one who misses out though, that's how I see it. The kids are really great. I'm spending the whole summer with them, until university starts again in February. It gives me a chance to save some money rather than paying it all out in rent. And I can help her at the same time."

"Are you working?"

"I found a job at the Black Cat Café. Just part time. I didn't want full time, since I'm helping Wanda out with the kids and housework. She's still full time, but I'm hoping she might be able to get some government assistance so she can pull back on the hours. She's so tired, what with the treatments and everything."

"How much longer does the treatment plan take?" Joanna asked.

"Only four more weeks. So, I can stay the entire time."

"Surely she could take those weeks off."

"I'm encouraging her to, but she wanted to save her leave for a holiday. I told her it would be sick leave, not vacation leave. I think she's going to submit a request."

"That's good. I'm glad she has you to help her with these things. It would be so overwhelming trying to manage it all alone."

"So, what are we making today?"

Joanna rubbed her hands together with glee. "We're going to make a Brunswick stew with corn bread. Some BBQ ribs. Macaroni and cheese. Green bean casserole. Honeyed carrots. Potato salad. Fried chicken, of course. And candied yams. I couldn't find yams, so I'm going to use sweet potatoes instead. Finally, we'll finish with banana pudding, peach cobbler and ice cream. Thankfully, peaches are in season and absolutely perfect this year."

"That sounds delicious. I can't say I've ever eaten most of those. So, I'm looking forward to trying them."

"You're going to love it. Everyone does. The southern states in America are renowned for their food. I visited once years ago, and I think I gained about five kilograms on the trip. I wanted to try everything." Joanna laughed. "But we can't do it all tomorrow, so I selected my favourites for our brunch. I'm going to make a pickled jalapeño sauce for anyone who wants to spice things up."

"I'm excited. Let's get started. I've got to get back in a few hours to help Wanda with bath and bedtime. I've promised she can sit in front of the television with a bucket of popcorn, and I'll take care of everything."

"I have an idea," Joanna said. "Let's make extra, and you can take some home for Wanda and the kids. That way, neither of you will have to cook dinner."

"Wonderful."

"I want most of the dishes to be fresh for tomorrow. But we can throw together the potato salad and corn bread, and I might also try out the fried chicken just to make sure my recipe is perfect."

"They'll love that," Emily replied.

"How are the wedding plans coming?" Joanna asked.

Emily poured beef stock into the slow cooker. "We haven't set a date yet. We want to wait until I've graduated."

"That's sensible. Do you know what kind of wedding you'd like to have?"

"I'm not sure. I thought something small and simple would suit us best. My family won't be helping pay for it, I know that. And I can't expect Aaron's family to foot the entire bill, so we'll be covering the expense ourselves. And even if we weren't, you know I'm not one to make a big fuss about anything. I just want to have the people who love us there, and that's all, really."

"I completely understand, honey. But just so you know, I've spoken to Gwen about it, and she's happy for the staff at the bistro to help me put together the catering."

"Really?" Emily grinned. "Oh, that would be amazing. It would really help us out."

"I'm happy to do it. And Gwen is a gem. She's always so generous."

"I'll thank her the next time I speak to her." Emily clapped her hands together. "I'm starting to get excited about it now. It feels so real."

"You should be excited. A girl only gets married once."

"That's the plan, at least," Emily replied.

Just then, Eva emerged from her bedroom with the baby in her arms. "Hey, Nan, I'm heading out."

"Are you going to the shops?"

"Yes, I need nappies and wipes. It's never-ending. I'm always running out."

Emily went over to see Gypsy, who was now nine months old. She held out a finger for the baby to hold and kissed her chubby cheek.

"Is she crawling yet?" Emily asked, unable to stop smiling. She loved babies and couldn't wait to have half a dozen of her own.

"She's been crawling for a few months, she's only doing that commando style. But Nan says not to worry—she'll figure out the other way when she's ready."

"Oh, I bet that's cute. I hope I can see her crawl before I leave."

"I'll be back soon," Eva said as she slid Gypsy into her pram and buckled her up. "Phew! She's getting heavy. I'm glad I don't have to carry her the whole way."

"Can you please get bread and milk while you're there?" Joanna asked, handing Eva a twenty.

"Sure, that's fine. Can I get ice cream too?"

"Of course you can, honey. But don't forget, we're cooking some of the dishes for the brunch today, so there'll be plenty of delicious food in the house."

"Oh, that's right. I don't have to come, do I?"

Joanna smiled. "No, you don't have to come. But you're welcome to if you'd like. Or you can take the food to your room, if that's what you prefer."

"Thanks, Nan." Eva leaned forward to kiss Joanna's cheek. "We'll be back soon."

"See you then."

Chapter Seven

Debbie Holmes reached one arm over her head and stretched. Then she leaned forward to touch her toes. The sand was cold beneath her, but the Pilates session had heated her up, and there was sweat trickling down the sides of her face.

"Thank you, everyone. We'll gather here again tomorrow at the same time. Keep up the good work. I see progress in all of you," the instructor said, standing up straight with a hand raised to shield her eyes from the rising sun.

Debbie stood to her feet and waved goodbye to the rest of the group. She rolled up her Pilates mat and then raised her arms over her head to work out the rest of the muscle fatigue that'd built up over the past few days. She wasn't as strong as she had been in the past. The challenges of her work environment had kept her preoccupied, and she hadn't done as much exercise as she usually would. The lack was showing up as pain in every muscle in her body now that she and Joanna had joined this morning Pilates class on Sunshine Beach a few days per week.

"I'll see you at the brunch," Joanna said as she tucked her mat under her arm.

The sun had inched its way up the sky and glimmered across the surface of a very still ocean.

"Yes, I'm looking forward to it. I'm bringing the mac and cheese, and I'm shocked at how much cheese I'm using. But it's all for a good cause." Debbie laughed.

Joanna looped one arm through Debbie's as they trudged back up the beach to the parking lot. "A very good cause, and I'm really looking forward to trying it. I love that you've embraced your inner cook since we wrote our book together."

"I'm never going to be as good as you. But I'm certainly better than I was." In fact, Debbie found that she enjoyed her time in the kitchen and had even taken some cooking classes down at the local TAFE college.

"You don't have to be a professional to enjoy it. And I love the food you make. I'm sure your husband is thrilled at this new hobby of yours."

"He's very excited about it," Debbie agreed. "Our entire marriage has been one of us throwing together a salad or something equally as simple, or ordering food. He's even started to take his BBQing more seriously and made some delicious kebabs the other night."

"That's good to hear. And how have you been coping with retirement?" Joanna stopped beside Debbie's car.

Debbie sighed. "I don't know. I'm not used to it yet. It's so strange—I don't have anything urgent to do with my time. I'm used to running on adrenaline, and I have no need for it any longer. But I'm keeping myself busy."

"Very busy, from what I've seen."

"Speaking of which, I've promised to deliver some food for Meals on Wheels this morning. So I'm off to do that, then I'll swing by the house and grab the mac and cheese and head over to your place for brunch."

"Aren't you volunteering at the Surf Life Saving Club as well?" Joanna asked.

"That's right—I'm keeping their books for them. It's temporary—the secretary is out with a gallstone. But she'll be back after her surgery, and I'll hand her the reins again."

"Well, I'll see you later. You really are Superwoman." Joanna laughed as she waved goodbye to walk back up the street to her house.

Debbie threw the Pilates mat in the back of her sports car, then climbed into the driver's seat and started the engine. She'd have to move quickly if she was going to get everything done on time, and she hated to be late. She accelerated backwards and heard a crunch, then threw on the brakes with a grimace.

Her heart in her throat, she looked in her rear vision mirror to see a large black SUV directly behind her. She inched the car forwards and climbed out.

"What on earth?" A middle-aged man with a balding pate walked towards her, his hands pressed to the sides of his head. "Why don't you watch where you're going?"

Debbie shook her head as she surveyed the damage to her fender. The SUV barely had a scrape on it, but her small sports car was badly damaged.

"Oh, no. I'm so sorry. I was in a hurry..."

"Well, slow down, lady. If you're in that much of a hurry that you can't check your mirrors, you're a danger to the rest of us."

Debbie didn't have time to argue with him, so she bit her tongue, swallowed down the irritation that climbed up her throat and threatened to spill out with sharp words, and handed him her insurance information.

"Do you want to call the cops?" he asked.

She shook her head. "Not unless you do. I'm in a hurry..."

"I think we already ascertained that."

"I'm so sorry."

"Just watch where you're going next time." He stormed

off and she watched him go, then climbed into her car and sped out of the parking lot, still fuming over the damage she'd done to her vehicle and grateful it wasn't worse.

* * *

After she'd delivered Meals on Wheels to three elderly men in the Sunshine area, Debbie hurried home. She only had half an hour before the brunch was due to start, and she hated to have her friends waiting on her. She pulled into the garage at the beach house and climbed out almost before she'd switched off the engine.

She burst through the doorway into the house and tripped on a box that'd been placed by the door.

"Whoa!" Her husband, Caleb, looked up from his bowl of cereal and the news he was reading on his iPad with concern on his face. "Are you okay? Where's the fire?"

She caught herself on a chair and managed to keep from falling to the floor. Then she righted herself and aimed for the kitchen. "I'm okay. Just in a hurry. The brunch starts soon. Speaking of which, are you coming today?"

"No, thanks," he replied. "You ladies have fun together. I'm going to play a round of golf."

He followed her into the kitchen and sidled up behind her, placing his hands around her waist and leaning in to kiss the side of her neck. She shook him off with a huff. "I don't have time, Caleb."

He stepped back, hands raised in the air. "Well, sorry! I just thought I'd say hello to my wife. I haven't seen you all morning. Where've you been, anyway?"

"I had Pilates, then I delivered some meals... I told you where I'd be last night." She felt frustrated. Sometimes it seemed like he never listened to her. No doubt he was busy playing on his phone.

"Oh, right. I forgot. You did mention that. Will I see you tonight?"

"I've got some work to do at the Surf Life Saving Club later, but we can have dinner…"

"More work? I thought you were supposed to slow down, but you're just as busy as you ever were. Retirement isn't supposed to be this stressful, Deb."

"How would you know?" she snapped, then immediately regretted her words. What was wrong with her? She was taking out her frustration on her husband, who had been nothing but kind and supportive to her. "I'm sorry. I didn't mean that."

He sighed. "Forget it. It's fine." He pressed his lips together.

"Oh, and I had a car accident this morning," she said as she hurried out of the kitchen with a casserole dish in her hands. She'd heat it up when she arrived. She didn't have time now.

"You what?" Caleb followed her.

"I reversed into someone at the beach. It's not a big deal. Just some damage to the bumper. It'll be fine."

"Debbie…"

She waved him off. "I've got to go. We can talk about it later. See you!"

He watched her leave from the garage. She poked an arm out the window to wave. She felt bad for snapping at him.

"You need to slow down and relax," he called out.

She grimaced. "I don't know how to relax."

"That's a problem, Deb!" he said, as she reversed down the driveway.

Chapter Eight

Beth decided to attend the monthly brunch at Joanna's house with her mother, Gwen. She didn't attend often, but she always enjoyed it when she did. The women were such good friends to her mother and had stuck with her through thick and thin. Besides that, Beth truly enjoyed their company. They were fun, happy and positive, and had always shown her love and kindness over the years.

As expected, the ladies had a million questions for her. She'd known them her entire life, and they always peppered her with queries about how she was going, who she was dating, what her plans were. She was used to it, and frankly, she kind of liked it. It was nice to know they cared.

"He broke up with you?" Debbie asked after swallowing a mouthful of Brunswick stew.

Beth was eating corn bread. She chewed with a nod.

"He's a..." Gwen hesitated with her wine glass halfway to her mouth. "Well, I don't like to name call. But you all know it's true. He's a... fill in the blank."

Joanna laughed. "You can name call, honey. We don't mind. And it seems to me that he probably deserves it."

Gwen sipped her wine. "And Beth has been a trooper."

"What will you do now?" Debbie asked. "Focus on your career?"

They were all seated around the dining table at Joanna's house. The food was delicious, and they were halfway through their meal before the subject of Brad's treatment of her came up for discussion. Beth was impressed it'd taken them that long, but they'd been busy discussing Debbie's driving skills, or lack of.

"My career has taken a hit as well," Beth replied with a sigh. She spooned more mac and cheese onto her plate.

"What's happened?" Debbie asked.

"I was fired."

"Oh, no," Joanna replied with a shake of her head. "I'm so sorry."

"That's horrible," Debbie added.

Emily filled Beth's glass with more white wine. "You've had a rough week, then."

"Very much so," Beth agreed. "The timing was terrible. I suppose maybe I could look at it differently— perhaps it was providential because now that I'm no longer working in the city, I could come back here to Sunshine to spend time with all of you. And I've really enjoyed being with Mum."

Gwen nodded, swallowing. "I've loved having you back."

"But I've got to find some work," Beth said. "I can't rely on your generosity forever."

"You could help me out with branding for the inn," Gwen said. "I've been meaning to get that done for a while and wanted to ask you about it. But I thought you were too busy with work and your life in the city. I'd love the help."

Beth smiled. "Of course, Mum. I'd be happy to do that for you, although I couldn't charge you for it. We're family, and I'm staying at your flat."

"Nonsense," Gwen replied with a huff. "I'm definitely

paying you. Your work is incredible, and you deserve to be paid well for it."

"Okay, thanks," Beth said.

"And the rest of us will keep our ears to the ground," Joanna added. "If we hear of any jobs, we'll let you know, but fair warning — we're hardly plugged into the graphic design scene."

"Thanks, everyone. I really appreciate your support. And it's so nice to be here with you, eating delicious food and having fun again. I've missed seeing you all."

"We've missed you too," Joanna replied.

"Oh, and my new dog is helping me readjust as well."

"New dog?" Debbie asked.

Gwen laughed. "Yes, it's great. My poor pup has had an invasion of his personal space. Beth found a stray dog in our hallway—who knows how on earth it got there? But no one in the building has claimed her, and the vet says she doesn't have a microchip. We've reported finding her to all the authorities but it looks like she's staying with us. At least for the short term."

"What a mystery," Joanna said. "At least you love dogs, Gwen."

"That's true," Gwen replied. "And she gets along well with my dog so far. The new doggo is happy to follow my pooch around the flat and has settled into the routine well."

"What are you calling her?" Debbie asked.

"I've come up with a really original name," Beth replied with a laugh. "She's white, so I called her Ivory."

"That's lovely," Joanna said.

Gwen huffed. "It's not so easy to call out at the dog park. *Ivory! Ivory!* I think she should simply revert it to Ivy, which is much easier to shout over and over. That dog doesn't listen. She obviously had an entirely different name she was used to responding to, and we just don't know what it is."

"I like the name," Beth replied with a defiant jut of her chin. "It goes well with Ebony. And besides, I think it suits her."

"Ebony and Ivory! How fun," Joanna said. "I just got that."

They all laughed. Then, they all dug into the meal accompanied by a few moments of silence.

"This mac and cheese is delightful, Debbie," Gwen said. "How did you make it?"

"Lots of different types of cheese," Debbie replied. "And I'm glad you like it. Thank you for the encouragement. I could use it."

"What's going on?" Gwen asked before taking another bite.

"I'm feeling a little lost, to be honest. I think I got more of my self-worth from running my own successful law firm than I realised. I don't know who I am now that it's gone."

Joanna frowned. "You're still you."

"I know that. But it's a deeper feeling — I'm unsettled. I don't quite know how to describe it, but I don't feel like I'm ready for retirement. I don't want to do nothing at all. All of you are still working, and now I'm the only one who isn't. And I don't have grandchildren like you do to keep me busy."

"I can understand that," Joanna replied. "You've felt valuable over the years because of the work you do. And that makes sense. You did fantastic work—you helped people and made a difference in the world. But you're still yourself without that work. I hope you know that we all value you immensely regardless of your career or what you do with your life."

"I know you do," Debbie replied. "But maybe I don't value myself enough."

Chapter Nine

When Gwen left the potluck brunch, it was late afternoon. She'd stayed longer than she had anticipated. Beth had left hours earlier to run some errands around town—Gwen wasn't exactly sure what. It was strange having her grown daughter living with her again after all these years. She found herself falling back into "mum" mode, asking questions and wanting to know where Beth was and what she was doing. But then she realised that her daughter was a grown adult and didn't need Gwen to supervise her lifestyle.

With a sigh, she climbed the stairs from the underground parking garage to her flat on the second floor. She walked down the hallway, already considering where she might take both of the dogs for their afternoon walk, but she felt enormously bloated. She'd have to fast tomorrow. Or maybe they should adjust their brunches to a lighter menu. She always overate at those things and made herself uncomfortable. But at least today she'd only had one glass of wine, so she was fine to drive home.

When she reached her flat, she saw there was a man sitting on the floor of the hallway, his back pressed to the door. Her heart thudded in her chest, and she was ready to turn and flee when she recognised him. It was her ex-husband, Duncan. His chin was resting against his chest. His legs were stretched out in front of him. He looked dead.

She felt terror rise up her throat, when he opened his eyes and looked up at her.

She pressed a hand to her chest. "Oh, Duncan, you scared the life out of me. What on earth are you doing?"

He fell to one side, laughing. "Oh, hey, Gwen-y. There you are. This door is locked."

She rolled her eyes. He was drunk. "Yes, I know it's locked. That's because it's my flat. And you don't live here."

"What? Why not? I'm your husband." He frowned and clambered to his feet. "I should have a key. Where's my key?"

"Ex-husband, Duncan. And may I remind you, that was your decision—you chose to have an affair and run off with a woman half your age. That wasn't my choice."

He leaned against the doorframe, then fell inwards when she opened it. He stumbled forwards and then righted himself.

The two dogs launched themselves at him, yapping. Ebony recognised him immediately and changed to keening as she wagged her tail. Ivory continued barking for a few moments. Duncan bent forward to pat her, and she stopped barking to wag her tail as well.

He propped himself up on a bar stool. Gwen was grateful —he looked as though he might topple over at any moment. "Now, don't be like that," he said. "You know I can't help what's happened. But that doesn't change the fact that we've been married for long time."

"I know, Duncan. Can I get you some coffee?"

"Anything harder than that?"

"Nope. Not for you. You need to sober up. Should I call your fiancée?"

He growled. "No. I'm not talking to her."

"Oh, trouble in paradise?" Gwen couldn't keep the sarcasm from her voice. It was true—she felt a little pleasure to know that he might be having difficulties in his new relationship with the Brazilian supermodel she'd seen him with. But she did want him to find happiness. Truly, she did. She would try to restrain herself from making any further sarcastic remarks.

He grunted. "She thinks I don't give her enough attention. I spend all my time trying to make her happy, and this is the thanks I get. More judgement, more criticism, more demands on my time. I'm a busy man. You know that!"

"I know that very well. You're right. I've dealt with your busy schedule for decades. So, I get it." She filled the kettle with water and set it to boil. "Have you explained to her that you like to work a lot?"

"I've told her how much my work means to me. That I've got to be there. No one else can fill my role. It's my business. I'm the boss. If I'm not there, the whole thing falls apart, and people are depending on me. Families are fed because I work hard to make sure that happens."

Gwen listened to him as she put biscuits onto a plate, and her heart squeezed. He'd never explained it to her this way before. He'd always simply flown into a rage if she questioned his long hours. "You feel responsible for your staff?"

"Of course," he slurred. "They need me to be there. Otherwise, business flounders and then I have to lay people off. What then? It hurts people. Remember that time we took the family to Fiji for two weeks?"

She nodded, handing him the plate of biscuits. He took a Tim Tam and bit into it.

"When I got back, we'd lost a big contract due to a miscommunication from one of the project managers, and I had to lay off five staff. I never forgot that."

"Why didn't you ever tell me?" Gwen asked before biting into a Tim Tam of her own.

He shook his head. "I didn't want to make you feel bad about taking a holiday. You worked hard too, taking care of the family. The business was my job, not yours. I didn't want to burden you with it."

Her throat tightened. If she'd known any of this, it might've changed her outlook. For so many years, she'd resented how much time he spent working. She'd thought they had enough money and didn't need more, that he was being greedy by pushing so hard when the business was already profitable. But it made sense that he was concerned about the other employees and their families.

"I'm sorry I wasn't more supportive."

He waved her off. "It's fine—I understood. You wanted me around more. I get it now. But at the time, it just made me mad. I was trying to keep you and the kids happy, keep the business afloat, make sure the employees were paid. It was hard to manage it all, and I felt as though you were ungrateful."

"Why couldn't we have just talked about this at the time?"

He shrugged. "I thought we did."

"No, we didn't. When I tried to address the subject, you'd get mad and yell at me."

"I did? Sorry about that. I can be a jerk at times. It's my stress reaction. At least, that's what my counsellor says."

"You're seeing a counsellor?" Gwen couldn't hide the surprise on her face. She wasn't merely surprised—she was shocked. She couldn't count the number of times she'd begged him to go to counselling and he'd refused. And now he was going, no doubt for his fiancée. It was infuriating, or at least it would've been if she let it get to her. But she was determined not to. They'd moved on—they were divorced. She had a new life, and it was a full one. She wasn't looking back. He'd simply break her heart all over again if she let him.

"Yep, I'm talking to her every week. She's pretty good. She says I have an anger reaction to stress, and I think she's probably right. So, I'm sorry about that. It wasn't fair on you. And I'm trying to do better—to come up with better coping mechanisms. Those are her words, obviously."

Gwen laughed softly and shook her head at him. It really was impossible to stay mad at him. "I'm glad you're getting some help."

He reached out a hand and laid it on her arm. "But I still need you, Gwen-y. You know I do."

"You have... what's her name?"

"She's not talking to me," he said, his brow furrowing.

"I thought you weren't talking to her."

"That's what I said," he replied. "And it's not the same. Not like it was with you. I was comfortable with you. It was home. Now I live in this sterile mansion, and there's no heart in it. It's not home to me. It doesn't feel right. And nothing I do is good enough for her. She wants more all the time. You were always happy with what I provided. You're a good wife. And I messed it up. Any chance you'd give me another go?"

He leaned forward with his lips puckered and bumped into her.

Gwen pushed him back gently with one hand on his chest. "You should go home, Duncan. You're drunk, and you're not thinking clearly. I'm sure you'll feel entirely differently tomorrow when you wake up with a sore head. I'm going to call you an Uber."

Chapter Ten

Joanna hung up the phone. Gwen had called to tell her that Duncan showed up drunk at her flat and asked her to take him back. She'd put him in an Uber en route to his fiancée a few minutes ago, then called Joanna to rant about the entire ordeal. Poor Gwen was feeling so confused over the whole matter, and just when she'd managed to pull her life together and move on. Joanna was more frustrated with Duncan than she could express, so she threw herself into cleaning up after their potluck brunch.

Most of the work had already been done by the group before they went home, but there were a few things to scrub that had been left to soak in the sink. Joanna put on gloves and got scrubbing. It helped ease her frustrations.

There was a knock at the door, and she had to remove her gloves so she could answer it. Chris was there, with a wrapped gift in his hands.

"Well, hello there."

He smiled. "I come bearing gifts."

"In that case, come on in," she said, waving him through the doorway.

She put the gloves back on and returned to her scrubbing. "Can I get you anything? I have a tonne of leftover food, if you're interested."

"I'm always interested in leftovers at your house," he replied as he picked up a tea towel and began drying the dishes she'd finished washing.

"Thank you," she said. "But you don't have to do that."

"I don't mind one bit. Aren't you curious about the gift?"

She sighed. "Oh, my goodness. I'm so sorry. Yes, of course I am. I'm distracted this afternoon, thinking about something Gwen told me. It's really rattled me."

She removed the gloves again and turned to face him. "This is kind of you."

He handed her the small package. She opened it and found a small box of chocolates and a gift card with *Extreme Indulgence* written on it.

"Chocolates! You know me well. And Extreme Indulgence? What is that?"

"It's a place that has massages and facials. That kind of thing. I thought it might be nice—a bit of indulgence never hurt anyone."

"That is so thoughtful. Why did you get me a gift?"

His cheeks grew pink. "Wasn't it your birthday last week?"

"Oh, yes, that's right. It almost slipped my mind. I don't really tell people about my birthdays, so it kind of whizzed by without me thinking much about it. Sixty-one isn't a particularly important milestone." She laughed, but it was hollow. The fact was, it had upset her a little that her family hadn't done much to celebrate other than a few text messages of congratulations. Eva hadn't even realised it was her birthday. But then again, her granddaughter had a lot going on, so Joanna could hardly hold it against her.

Chris laughed. "You forgot your own birthday? Well, I

didn't forget. But as you know, I was away at my son's place last week, so I couldn't give you this until now."

"How was your trip?" Joanna asked. She set the gift aside and returned to her scrubbing.

"It was nice. We had a good catch-up. They're doing well. Keeping busy, of course. It's that time of life. Isn't it?"

"It certainly is."

Finally, she finished scrubbing pots. Chris dried the last one. Then she made him a plate of food. She was still full, but she fixed them both a cup of tea to go with it. They went and sat out in the sunroom to watch the sun set. It was a brilliant display of colours in the clear, darkening sky, and she was over-awed again by the majesty of nature. It never ceased to amaze her.

"Don't you love sunsets?" she gushed.

He swallowed a mouthful of stew. "I love a good sunset, but not as much as I love this food. You've really done a great job."

"Thank you. I'm glad you like it. It was a team effort— Gwen did the decorations and made a banana pudding for dessert. Debbie made the mac and cheese, and Emily helped with everything else."

"You're an amazing team. You could open a restaurant. Oh, wait!...In fact, I ate at the bistro recently, and it was delightful. Different to this, of course, since it serves French cuisine, but still delicious."

"We don't all work there, obviously. But I put the menu together, and chose and trained the kitchen staff. The rest is Gwen. She's done a marvellous job of building the team and making everything work. I don't know how she has the energy, to be honest, she said she's just hired a new concierge who has a lot of experience. That should help relieve a little bit of the pressure going forward. At least, I hope so."

"A new concierge? I don't think I met anyone new," Chris said around a mouthful of corn bread.

"Yes, she only hired her recently. Apparently, the poor woman's husband died while they were staying at the inn, and she didn't have anywhere else to go. There's some intrigue there, and I'd love to get to the bottom of it. I have so many questions."

"Very curious," Chris agreed. "I'm sure we'll get to meet her soon and form our own opinions."

"I hope so. I love a good mystery. I know I shouldn't be nosy, but I can't help myself." Joanna wrinkled her nose. "It's just who I am."

Chris laughed. "I happen to like who you are."

"I like you just as much, I assure you," Joanna replied, feeling warm inside. Chris always encouraged her and made her feel good. He was like a ray of sunshine in her life, and she was glad they'd gotten to know each other better recently.

"Speaking of which..." he said.

She took a sip of tea, nodding.

"I wanted to ask you something."

"Ask away."

"Would you like to have dinner with me sometime?"

"We're having dinner right now," she said with a chuckle.

"No, I mean—go out together, on a date. My treat."

Her heart skipped a beat. "Oh."

"So, what do you say?"

"I think that would be lovely."

"Yes?"

"Yes, let's do that." Joanna shifted uncomfortably in her chair. It felt suddenly hotter in the sunroom that it had previously.

"Great. How about next Friday? I'll swing by and pick you up around six."

"Next Friday is perfect."

Before things could become any more awkward, Eva appeared in the sunroom doorway. She wore a shift dress that showed off her slim physique, which had returned to normal very quickly after Gypsy was born. However, there was a maturity in Eva's eyes that hadn't been there before. She'd grown a lot as a person and a mother in the past nine months.

"Hi, Nan," she said. "I hope I'm not interrupting."

"Not at all, honey. Come on out if you like. Chris is having some of the leftovers, and there's plenty more if you're hungry."

"I think I'll grab a plate in a minute. I wanted to tell you something."

"Oh?" Everyone seemed to have something big to announce today. She was still getting over the shock of Chris's invitation. She braced herself for whatever Eva was about to say.

"I've enrolled in distance education for year eleven. I can do it from home. That way, I won't have to leave the baby or put her in daycare. And I'll be able to graduate a year after that, only one year later than I would've without having Gypsy." She swallowed and twisted her hands together, watching Joanna for a reaction.

Joanna offered her a wide smile. "That is wonderful news, honey. I hadn't even thought of that, but what a fantastic solution to our problem. Well done. You're becoming so mature."

"What a great idea," Chris agreed.

Eva grinned and clapped her hands together. "Yay! You like it. I'm gonna call Mum and tell her."

As she bounced out of the room, Joanna couldn't stop grinning. "That was a miracle. We've been fighting about her finishing high school for months."

Chris shook his head from side to side. "Sometimes they just surprise you in the best ways. Don't they?"

"They certainly do."

Chapter Eleven

The car was at the mechanic's, and Debbie was bored. She was stuck at home with nothing to do. She should've hired a rental, but the work was only supposed to take a few hours. Instead, it was mid-afternoon, and the car still wasn't done, which meant Debbie had to find something else to fill her day other than the planned trip to the Surf Life Saving Club to work on their accounts.

The previous day, she and Caleb had attended church together. Then he'd returned to Brisbane that morning for work. He wasn't sure yet whether he intended to spend the night at their condo or return to Sunshine to stay with her. But if her car still wasn't ready to collect at close of business, she might well have another day at home alone with nothing to do.

She stood at the window, staring out at the neighbourhood. There was a strong wind blowing, which made the heat more bearable even though she had the air-conditioning blasting, since she hated to spend the day bathed in her own sweat. Still, she hoped the wind wouldn't take down any trees. There were a few around their boundary line that could land on the house if they fell. Perhaps she should get them trimmed to prevent something like that from happening. She hated to get them removed, since they really were beautiful tall gum trees, likely decades old. But gums were notorious for losing branches and falling in strong winds, and that could be dangerous.

She flicked through her phone, looking for a tree felling company, but something out the window caught her eye. It was a neighbour. At least, she thought it was. A man strode around the outside of the house next door, walked into the garage and was hidden from view for a few moments. Then stepped backwards out of the doorway. The door was open and faced out towards Debbie's living room. There was a large truck parked in the centre of the garage, filling up most of the space. He pulled something heavy behind him. It bumped down the stairs into the garage.

Debbie leaned forwards, squinting, her palms pressed to the wall on either side of the window. What was he pulling? It looked awkward, and as though it weighed him down. He was tugging hard to inch it over the concrete floor. Then he disappeared behind the truck, and she saw the vehicle's tyres sag as though something heavy had been placed into the bed.

She frowned. That was strange. The heavy item had been encased in a blanket or fabric bag of some kind. She couldn't tell from where she was sitting, but it looked suspiciously like a body. It couldn't be, of course. She was simply letting her imagination run wild, but it had seemed that way. And her neighbour was just the type, if anyone cared for her opinion on the matter. He was middle-aged, with a thick beard. His arms were muscular, his thighs like tree trunks. And whenever she walked by his house and waved hello, he rarely smiled, but simply raised a palm in greeting. His face remained expressionless. Who did that? Maybe he was a sociopath who'd just murdered someone. His wife, perhaps?

No, she was imagining things. People didn't murder their wives in Sunshine. It wasn't done. This community never experienced crime. There was no violence in the village. It was a peaceful, happy place where everyone knew each other.

She wandered into the kitchen and boiled water in the kettle. While she waited, her fingernails drummed on the kitchen bench, increasing with speed as each second passed. Then she poured the hot water into a cup and added tea encased in a strainer. She waited for it to steep while she sliced a piece of sourdough loaf and slathered it with butter. Then she carried her tea and bread to the porch, set them on a small, round table, and took a seat in one of a pair of rocking chairs she'd ordered from a craftsman on the eastern side of the island. She rocked for a few minutes, watching the neighbours' house closely.

The truck pulled out of the darkened garage, the door whirring shut behind it. The windows were tinted, so she couldn't see more than an outline of her neighbour. She raised a hand in greeting, but he didn't seem to respond. Then he pulled out of the driveway and turned onto the road that headed for the state park—a remote area, covered in thick brush and vegetation that backed onto a pair of long, golden beaches rounding the end of the island.

She peered after it, then reached for her tea and took a sip. It was nothing. He was no doubt going four-wheeling or maybe taking a hike. There were a dozen different reasons he might visit the state park in the late afternoon. Nothing to worry about. Nothing at all. Her heart jittered against her ribcage. Maybe she should check on his wife. Debbie hadn't lived on the island in years. She wasn't as familiar with the islanders as Joanna and Gwen were. She wasn't certain of her neighbour's names—Tim and Carol? No, Anna. It was Anna, she was fairly certain. Maybe she should knock on the door and make sure Anna was okay.

She set her teacup back on the table and slipped on a pair of sandals by the back door. Then she trotted over to the neighbours' front door. Their yard was neat, but in need of a trim. Their garden was simple, if a little overgrown. The house was a single-story brick structure with a dark, peaked roof. She stood at the front door for a moment, heart hammering in her chest. Then she pressed the doorbell. It rang loudly through the house, a melodic sound muffled only by the shut door.

There was no movement inside. She waited a moment and pressed her hands to the glass pane next to the door to peer inside. An entrance. A hall table with a vase of dead flowers. An umbrella stand. A pair of joggers. And in the distance, the edge of what looked to be a living area. She could just see the side of a piano.

It seemed no one was home. She tried the doorbell again, then knocked. Still nothing. A cat crouched in the garden beside her and gave her a fright. It hissed at her, and she raised her hands in mock surrender.

"I'm not going to hurt you. I promise."

The cat hissed again, and she hurried back to her own house. Where was Anna? Or was it Carol? She really should get to know her neighbours better now that she was spending most of her time at the beach house. She might need to borrow a cup of sugar or something, whatever it was neighbours needed from one another. And she should know their names at the very least. She would make it a priority just as soon as she had the chance and Anna was at home.

Back on her porch, she called Caleb. Then she paced up and down the porch, watching the neighbours' house as the phone rang.

"Hey, honey," she said.

"Oh, hi, Deb. How's your day going?"

"The car *still* isn't ready."

"I guess it's going to take a little longer than they said, huh?"

"It's so frustrating. I've been stuck at home all day long. And it's just about closing time, so I'm sure I won't get it back until tomorrow."

"I wish I could tell you I was coming home, but I won't make it tonight. I'm going to stay in the city. You don't mind. Do you?"

She continued pacing. "I don't mind. Only…"

"What is it?"

"Something's bothering me about the neighbours."

"Which ones? Wayne and Kim, or Tim and Anna?"

She was right—it *was* Anna. How did Caleb know their names, but she didn't?

"Tim and Anna."

"What about them? Are they okay?"

She studied the neighbours' house. If only she had a pair of binoculars. That might help her peep through the windows. It was getting dark now, and she probably wouldn't be able to see much. She remembered stashing some binoculars in the office. They'd used them once for whale watching.

"I was in the dining room, looking out of the window, when I saw Tim drag something heavy out to his truck. It was wrapped in a blanket. I'm worried it was a body. Anna's body." She whispered the sentence, as though Tim might leap out from behind the hedges at any moment.

Caleb was quiet on the other end of the line.

"Hello?" she said.

Caleb chuckled softly. "You think our neighbour, the paramedic who works long shifts to save people's lives, has killed his wife in the middle of the day and dragged her body out to his truck while you were watching? Really?"

"When you put it like that... it sounds silly."

"Honey, I think you need to find something to do while you're at home. Something other than spying on the neighbours."

She huffed. "It looked suspicious."

"I'm sure it did because you don't know what he was doing. But really, you shouldn't be snooping. And clearly, you're bored because your car isn't there and you can't get out and do the million things you normally would."

"You're right, I'm bored. And now that I say it out loud, it's ridiculous. Of *course* he wouldn't kill his wife and dispose of her body in the daylight like that."

"I really don't think he would."

"Thanks, honey."

"You should put your feet up and read a book or watch a movie. You never get to do things like that. And now is your chance."

"That *would* be nice. I might do that."

"Okay, well, be good and don't go getting into any mischief while I'm gone. I won't be there to rescue you."

She laughed, feeling the tension dissipate. What was she thinking? She could always count on Caleb to help her back to reality if her imagination carried her away. It didn't make sense that her neighbour was a murderer. She should probably stop binge-watching murder mysteries at night before bed. It made her paranoid.

They spoke for a few more minutes before she hung up the phone. He wasn't coming home, so she decided to make herself a baked beans and cheese toasted sandwich for dinner. Simple, delicious, and it didn't require the use of any dishes other than one small plate and the toasted sandwich maker.

With her sandwich and a glass of wine, she sat in the media room and flicked on the television, then found a thriller. Tomorrow she would give up on crime shows, but she wanted to watch one last movie tonight. She tucked her feet up beneath her and took a sip of wine with a glance in the direction of the neighbours' house at the sound of a door slamming. It was none of her business. Likely Tim had come home. But it didn't matter to her—she had a movie to watch.

Chapter Twelve

The branding for the inn didn't take Beth very long. She found that the ideas flowed freely and easily. She loved her mother's inn. It was a beautiful place full of character, smooth lines and stylish décor. The brand was easy to develop—it was chic but with a retro feel to it. After a little while, she had all the files worked out and ready to send to her mother as a first draft.

She sent off the email and then spent an hour looking through job advertisements. As nice as it was to work on the branding for the inn, it was a small job, and she needed something full time or she wouldn't be able to pay the bills. She still lived with her mother, but she couldn't do that forever. She was closing in on thirty—at least, she would in two years' time. It was hard to believe that her twenties were almost over. It felt as though she'd only graduated from university a minute ago.

After applying for five different positions around Southeast Queensland, she closed up her computer and set it aside. She made herself a sandwich for lunch, along with a fruit smoothie. Her mum had bought an entire tray of mangoes, so she had one after her sandwich and enjoyed letting the juice drip from her chin to the plate below as she ate. It was delicious.

She cleaned up and then called Jemma, her best friend. They'd become friends in year seven and had remained close ever since.

"Hi, Jemma."

"Well, if it isn't the wandering stranger who used to be my best friend." Jemma's teasing tone gave her away.

Beth laughed. "I'm sorry. I've been slack."

"A bird told me you were back in town. But I said, there's no way my bestie would come back to Sunshine without telling me."

"I needed some time to myself. I'm sorry. But I was hoping you might be up for a swim this afternoon."

"I'd love a swim. Want to meet on Sunshine Beach?"

"Yes, please. By the rock pools."

"Perfect. When?"

"Now?"

"I'll see you in half an hour."

Beth hung up the phone with a smile on her face. She could always count on Jemma to be there for her, even if she pretended to be put out by Beth's slack communication skills. She dressed in a bikini and white linen coverup. Then she donned a wide-brimmed straw hat and a pair of thongs. She was walking distance from the rock pools, so there was no need to get her car out of the garage. She said goodbye to the dogs, and then strode to the lift.

The beach was still, with only a light breeze. The waves were small and glinted under the bright afternoon sunlight. Seagulls hovered overhead, cawing as they tipped their heads to one side to watch Beth walking, curious to see if she carried food.

Beth's blonde hair was pulled back into a ponytail, and her blue eyes were hidden behind a pair of large black sunglasses.

She applied suncream as she walked, then returned the tube to the fabric bag slung over her shoulder.

Jemma was already there waiting for her, wearing a bright blue bikini and her black hair tucked up beneath a peaked cap. Her lithe figure was trim and tanned from running triathlons, and she grinned when she saw Beth approaching. She ran over to hug Beth, squeezing her and lifting her off her feet.

Beth laughed. "You're crushing my ribcage."

"And you deserve it. I can't believe you're back on the island. I assume you're living with Gwen?"

"That's right," Beth replied. "But it's temporary. I'm unemployed and single."

Jemma's smile faded. "I heard about the boyfriend, but not the job. Why didn't you tell me?"

"I couldn't. It's been hard to talk about. Feels like my whole life is falling apart at the same time."

"Are you okay?" Jemma asked, sympathy written across her pretty face.

"I'll be fine. I'm stronger than I look." She bit down on her lower lip. "I'm good, actually. Just feeling a little sorry for myself. I'm twenty-seven, almost twenty-eight and I'm single again. I'm starting to wonder if I'll ever get married and have children."

They walked side by side down to the water's edge, and Beth put her feet in. The water was colder than she'd expected, and she inhaled a gasp.

"You've never really talked about kids."

"I know. I guess I assumed I'd have them. I'm not one of those women who dream about it, or pine for them. But now that there's a prospect of not finding someone, and not having them, it's freaking me out."

"You're not even thirty yet," Jemma said. "Why would you be worrying about that now?'

"Easy for you to say. You've got a wonderful husband."

"I am lucky," Jemma replied. "But you didn't really see Brad as *the one*, did you?"

"I don't know. I suppose not. Not really. But I hoped maybe he would turn out to be the one."

"If he was the one, you'd know it."

"Do you think so?"

"Absolutely," Jemma replied with an emphatic nod of the head. "Like with Dan and me. We fell in love within a few weeks of our first date. I knew I wanted to marry him right away, and he said the same. Did you feel that way with Brad?"

"No, not really. I liked him, and he seemed keen on me. But I guess it wasn't that kind of head-over-heels love you're talking about. I do want that. I'm not sure I'm going to find it —that's the problem."

They walked back up the sand and found a place to lay their bags. Then Beth pulled off her coverup, hat, and sunglasses, slipped out of her sandals, and they ran down the beach to leap over the waves. They swam in the ocean for an hour, enjoying the rise and fall of the waves and the warmth of the sun on their faces and shoulders. The water was clear and cool. Not so cold as it had been at first, but perfect for the hot day.

Afterwards, they spread out their towels in the sand and lay on them. Beth covered her face with her hat and enjoyed the feel of the sun drying her body.

"Hey, do you remember that boy I met here on the beach at New Year's when we were thirteen?" Beth asked suddenly.

Jemma propped herself on one elbow to look at Beth, who squinted at her beneath her hat brim. "Do you mean Damien?"

Beth laughed. "You remember his name? Wow. Good memory."

"It's not difficult to recall the name you scrawled all over everything you touched in Grade Eight. You wrote Damien everywhere, surrounded by love hearts. You were sickening, really. Honestly, I wanted to heave."

"Okay, it wasn't that bad."

"Oh, yes, it was."

"Well, anyway, he and I said that if we were both single at twenty-eight, we'd meet up here on the beach on New Year's Eve. Just like we did that night."

"Yeah, that's right. I forgot about that part of it." Jemma sighed. "It's kind of romantic when you think about it now."

"I wonder what his life has been like," Beth said. "I think about him all the time."

"You do?"

"More so lately, ever since Brad broke up with me. But yes, over the years, I've thought about him every now and then. What kind of man has he become? Has he ever thought about me? What he's doing with himself? Does he remember our pact?"

"Mmm." Jemma lay down again.

"It's this year."

"What's this year?"

"We're twenty-eight this year, so it's been fifteen years. I'll have my birthday right before New Year's."

"Oh, yeah, of course. It *is* this year. Do you think he'll show?"

Beth pondered this question. The truth was, she didn't think so. It'd been too long. There was no way he remembered their tryst the way she did. She had too vivid an imagination. He couldn't have felt the same way she did, although he seemed to at the time, and he told her so. But it was years ago. Too much time had passed since then.

"Are you going to the New Year's festival here on the beach?" Jemma asked.

Beth sat up and righted her hat on her head. She crossed her arms over her knees and looked up and down the beach.

This beach was where she'd grown up. She'd spent every summer here for as long as she could remember. It was home to her in a way outsiders would never understand.

"I'll be here."

Jemma sat up too and stared at her. "Really?"

"Yep. If there's a chance he *will* show up, I have to be here. Right?"

"Absolutely," Jemma said.

"But it's not likely."

"No, of course it's not likely. But the odds aren't zero."

"Better than zero. That's something." Beth gave her a crooked smile. "I'm pathetic."

"No, you're romantic."

"Is that the same thing?"

Jemma laced an arm around Beth's shoulders. She leaned in to press her cheek to Beth's. "Definitely not."

Chapter Thirteen

Two weeks later, Gwen was at the inn and feeling very happy with herself. The new concierge, Francesca, was working out even better than she'd hoped. Francesca had gone home to bury her husband and pack up her house. Then she'd found a place to rent in Sunshine, moved here, and was living on folding furniture and an inflatable mattress until her things arrived on the moving truck.

Meanwhile, she had started work at the inn two days ago alternating between concierge and day manager, when Mallory wasn't rostered, and already she had whipped the staff into shape in a way that Gwen had only dreamed of. They listened to Francesca, did what she asked, and the entire place was running like clockwork. It was a huge load off Gwen's shoulders, and she'd been surprised at how quickly Fran had settled into the role.

Things were winding down for the day. Every room was filled with guests. The dinner service was over, with the restaurant in clean-up mode. Fran was checking that everything was ready for the next day before she headed home. She stood at the reception counter, looking over the following day's reservation and check-out list.

Gwen sat in the small office behind her. She closed her email and shut down the computer, then stretched her neck by rolling her head to one side, then the other. With a yawn, she picked up her purse and headed out, locking the office door behind her.

"You should go home," Gwen said to Fran. "It's getting late."

Fran looked up. There were dark smudges beneath her eyes. She seemed sad. Gwen's heart ached for her and what she'd been through.

"I'm okay. The flat is a bit empty right now. I'd rather be here, honestly."

Gwen glanced at her watch. She wanted nothing more than to go home and put her feet up—she'd been on them all day. But she hated to leave Fran feeling like this.

"Do you want to grab a drink before we head out?"

"That sounds nice."

Gwen found a bottle of Scotch in the kitchen, poured them each some over ice, and carried the two glasses out onto the large deck behind the restaurant. The sound of the waves crashing against the nearby beach was soothing. It was one of Gwen's favourite things, to sit and listen to the ocean.

Gwen handed Fran a drink.

Fran raised her glass. "To new friendships."

"And new beginnings," added Gwen as they clinked their glasses together.

They drank and sat in silence for a few moments.

"How is your new place working out?" Gwen asked.

"It's fine. It's a lovely little cottage by the ocean. I've always wanted something like that. And I decided to buy it because it was on the market for a reasonable price."

"Good for you."

"Marco would've loved it, but he didn't want to buy. Said it was a waste of freedom. He liked to move about—he didn't want to be stuck in one place."

"What about you? Do you like to stay put?"

Fran shrugged. "I never thought about it much before. Marco was a force of nature. He always got his way, so I gave in. I was the water moving around the rock, and he was the rock. But now that he's not here, I feel differently—I want to stay. I like the idea of putting down roots and having a place to call home. I don't want to rent any longer. And this is as good a place as any for me to set up a life for myself. I like it here. And I learned from my solicitor that I have enough money to buy many beachside cottages, if I want them."

"I'm glad to hear that," Gwen replied. "Good for you. I'm so happy you're staying. You've been a lifesaver. I don't know what I would've done if you hadn't shown up. I couldn't keep managing everything myself. I'm too old for all that." She chuckled. "So, thank you for coming to Sunshine. I'm sorry the circumstances were so awful for you though."

"Thank you—I appreciate that. I've felt very welcomed, and I'm enjoying your inn. You've built a lovely place here. I can see it becoming a fixture in the tourist industry for the area."

"I hope you'll help me with that. I can definitely use advice from a veteran of the industry, since I'm new to it all." Gwen often felt completely overwhelmed by what she'd chosen to take on with the inn and the bistro. But so far, she'd managed to keep her head above the water line.

"I'll help you in any way I can. Does your husband have any involvement in the business?"

Gwen hesitated. She didn't like bringing up Duncan, especially not since his recent visit to her flat. She was still pondering what it'd meant. She'd been hard on him, maybe too hard. She didn't like pushing him away, but she wasn't sure what else to do. He'd divorced her. Or had she divorced him? Either way, he'd rejected her to spend his time and energy and love on another woman. And now he had the hide to want her back? It was unfair the way he was toying with her heart.

"Duncan isn't involved, and we're divorced."

"I'm sorry to hear that. Is it recent?"

"Yes, very recent. In fact, the divorce is the reason I have the money and inclination to take on the inn and restaurant and make them what I have. Otherwise, I'd be at home looking after grandchildren, like I've done for years."

"Do you regret it?"

"Not one little bit," Gwen mused, realising that it was true. "I did something that was scary. I didn't know how to go about it. And I managed it all on my own. I'm proud of myself. I don't know how long I'll keep going with it. After all, I'm close to retirement age, and this place wears me out. But for now, I'm loving it. And it has given me a new outlook, a new motivation to keep going each day. I get up with a smile on my face—and with some very sore muscles at times."

Fran laughed, and Gwen considered that it was the first time she'd seen her really smile. She had a very pretty smile. It lit up her entire face.

"I can understand that. I'm exhausted already, since I haven't worked in years. But I wouldn't want to do anything else with my time right now."

"You know, you have a very familiar face. I feel like I've seen you before somewhere."

"Have you ever been to Italy?"

Gwen frowned. "Yes. Why?"

"I used to feature in tourism videos, brochures, photographs. They used my face a lot for their campaigns. They found me in a resort in Florence, where I was working as a housekeeper at the time."

"You're right—that's where I've seen you. I remember you clearly now. It's the eyes—they're the same. They give you away."

Fran smiled serenely. "It was a long time ago."

"And were you born in Italy?"

"Yes, that is my home, but I haven't lived there in many years. One of my daughters, our eldest, lives there. But after that, we did a stint in Dubai, so our son chose to stay there. We're a very scattered family. Our final stop has been Australia, and this is where I've chosen to stay."

"And how are they going with the investigation into your husband's death?" Gwen asked.

Fran sighed. "They say he died of a stroke."

"I'm so sorry."

"Thank you. And now I can move forward with my life."

"Yes, you can," Gwen replied with a sympathetic smile. "It's hard to do at first, but you'll get there."

Chapter Fourteen

After five outfit changes, Joanna finally settled on a pair of grey slacks and a white blouse for her first date with Chris. It felt strange to think of them going on a date together. She'd known Chris forever. They'd attended high school together. Most probably primary as well, although she'd have to get out her old school photographs to confirm that. They weren't friends in high school, although she vaguely recalled seeing him around, and they'd been in the band together.

Then each of them had gone off to university, gotten married, had a family and moved back to Bribie Island at some point. They'd lived next door to one another for years, and Chris had known her husband back before he passed. They'd probably even played golf together at some point, and as couples they'd had backyard BBQs on occasion. But now that both of them had lost their spouses, they'd become friends. Good friends. And she valued his friendship more than she could've imagined.

Would a date ruin that?

She didn't want to change their relationship. They were neighbours. It might be awkward. But what if it could be great? What if he could be the person she spent her golden years with? It was a distinct possibility—they got along well. She was attracted to him as a very handsome man. He'd always been good-looking with those piercing blue eyes.

She fixed a silver necklace with a circle pendant around her neck, then touched up her makeup. With one last glance in the bathroom mirror, she padded in stockinged feet to the closet to search for a pair of shoes. She wasn't sure where he was taking her, but comfort was her most important criteria for footwear these days. The time of teetering down the street on impossibly high heels was long behind her. Now all she wanted was something that wouldn't give her blisters or make her plantar fasciitis play up.

The final touch was a spray of perfume. Then she selected a purse and headed for the kitchen. She'd sip a glass of wine in front of the television while she waited, since she was ready a little early. She hated to be rushed, so early suited her just fine.

He arrived promptly at seven, like he'd promised, and escorted her to the car with a hand resting gently on the small of her back. It made her feel young and beautiful again. And she liked the tingle of adrenaline that came with the prospect of what was to come.

"You look lovely," Chris said as he opened the car door for her.

"Thank you. You're very handsome yourself." He wore a pair of chinos with a buttoned-down blue shirt that brought out the colour in his eyes and a pair of comfortable loafers. His grey hair was neatly combed to one side.

They chatted about the weather and about their respective weeks as they drove. Then Chris pulled into the local mini putt-putt course. Joanna was pleasantly surprised.

"I haven't played mini golf in forever. I can't remember the last time."

He laughed. "I thought you probably hadn't, and it's

always a fun time. Plus, it's almost playing golf, which you know I love."

"And I can't stand..."

"I knew that. So, this is the next best thing."

He was right—they did have fun. Joanna was a terrible shot and had a very off-kilter golf swing, but she had some lucky shots, and by the last hole, she was two strokes ahead of Chris. A minor miracle, in her opinion.

He stood behind her and reached around her waist to adjust her grip on the stick. "Here you go. This should make it a little easier for you to take aim."

"Thank you," she said as goose bumps appeared on her arms. Having him so close stirred something up inside of her she hadn't felt in years.

He smiled as she watched him, then stepped back to let her take the shot. She sent the ball hurtling through a spinning wheel, but it ricocheted off a windmill and ran back down the hill again. She grunted. "Ugh, so much for that. You're going to beat me. I can just tell."

"I could let you win..."

"Don't you dare," she threatened.

He laughed. "As you wish."

Her favourite movie was *The Princess Bride*. He knew that because he'd watched it with her at least three times over the years. She smiled at his back as he swung the stick. The ball went through the windmill and came to rest beside the hole.

"I told you. If you win, you owe me a drink."

"Deal," he replied.

Of course he won. He knocked the ball in with the next put, and she took five more swings to get hers into the hole. So, he walked with her to the bar and purchased a glass of wine each. They sat on a deck overlooking the course and ate an appetiser platter of crackers, cheese and olives while they drank their wine.

"This is lovely," Joanna said. "I've never been here. I didn't realise how nice it is."

"And they have a full golf course as well. I'm a member of the club. I don't expect you to join me, though. The putt-putt is for the family members who don't want to use the eighteen-hole course."

"Perfect for me," she said.

"And there's a gym with a sauna, spa and swimming pool. I think they even have water aerobics. Or you can swim laps, if that's what you prefer."

"Better and better. I'm perfectly content to take a dip, sit in the sauna and sip wine while you play golf." Then her cheeks reddened as she realised she'd just assumed they would do this again and invited herself on a date with him.

But he seemed pleased with that and nodded his head. "I hoped you'd say that. Caleb has a membership here as well, and we often play together. I'm sure Debbie would love to spend some time here with you."

"Oh, how wonderful. That would be lovely. I might get a membership myself."

"You know, I'm amazed at how confident you are this year. Last year, you were still struggling to get out of the house. I hope you don't mind me talking about it."

"Not at all. I'm glad to talk about it. If we keep things hidden in the darkness, they'll fester and grow. It was when I started talking about my issues that I found I could deal with them, and they weren't so overwhelming or scary any longer. If I hadn't brought them out into the light, I would probably still be stuck at home, wishing I could get out and about."

"You're an amazing woman. Most people don't have this kind of insight into themselves, or the strength to do anything about their struggles."

"You were a big part of that," Joanna said. "You always encouraged me. You enticed me with the prospect of taking walks on the beach with you. It helped me have the motivation to push myself."

"I'm glad I could do something to help," Chris said with a twinkle in his eye. "Cheers to spurring each other on."

They clinked glasses together and drank without breaking eye contact. Something special passed between them. Something unspoken. A spark of electricity, an understanding, a knowing of one another that was only for the two of them. It sent a thrill down her spine.

He took her to an Italian restaurant for dinner after that, and the food was magnificent. She had the veal parmigiana, and he ordered the tortellini. She tried his, and he tasted hers. They had another glass of wine each and laughed more than she had in a long time.

When he dropped her home, she wondered if he would kiss her. He walked her to her door, then stopped to watch her fumble with her keys.

"I had a nice time," she said as she slid a key into the lock and turned it.

She spun to face him, her face burning, her lips tingling in anticipation. How long since she'd been kissed? Before her husband died. Years ago. She wished she could recall their last kiss, but it'd been so commonplace for them, she hadn't seared it into her memory. They'd kissed every day. Every time they saw one another. It was such a normal part of her life, it seemed strange now that it'd been over a decade since his lips had been on hers.

And now Chris was there, standing in front of her, about to lean in and kiss her in that same way. Only he wasn't Ron. His lips would be different, and the excitement of knowing that made her pulse race.

Chris placed his hands on each of her arms and bent forward, his lips hovering over hers. She quivered beneath his touch and let her eyes drift shut, waiting. Then his lips brushed against her cheek.

"Thank you, Jo. I had a great time with you. We should do it again sometime."

"Oh, yes. Thank you for a lovely evening."

He turned to walk back down her driveway to his own, waving. She opened the front door and stepped inside, shutting off the outside light. Disappointment flooded through her. Why hadn't he kissed her? She'd been waiting—had tilted her head towards him, closed her eyes, but he'd kissed her cheek. Had she done something wrong?

"You look like a guilty teenager," said a voice in the darkness.

"Eva, you startled me," Joanna said with a jump.

The kitchen light flared to life. Eva held an empty baby bottle in her hand and laughed. "Young lady, if I catch you making out in front of the house again, I might have to ground you."

Joanna groaned. "Heavens! If only. No kiss for me, it seems."

"Sorry, Nan. That sucks."

She smiled. "You're right. It does suck."

Chapter Fifteen

In the almost ten months since Debbie had closed the door at her law firm, she'd focused her energy and attention on learning new skills. She'd learned to cook and to speak French and Japanese, albeit badly. She was taking an art class to learn how to paint in water colour. She'd taken up gardening. The garden at their beach house had never looked so good. And she'd built a large kitchen garden behind the house hidden away from view since they lived in an up-market area, and she suspected the neighbours didn't want to see her pumpkin patch from their driveway.

Speaking of the pumpkin patch . . . She pulled at a stray vine with her gloved hands. It came free, and she almost landed on her rear end in the damp dirt. She stumbled and caught her balance. The pumpkin vine had decided to invade the entire yard and take over as much ground as it could manage. If she didn't trim it back, she'd end up with pumpkins stacked from there to the front curb. There was no way the two of them could ever eat so much pumpkin, even if she managed to convince everyone they knew that pumpkin soup was just the thing for autumn. Thankfully, the pumpkins hadn't grown yet, but that time was coming, and so she pulled out her secateurs to prune it back.

A short tap on a car horn in the driveway caught her attention. She adjusted her straw hat and tramped around the side of the house to find that Joanna had arrived unannounced. She loved when her friends dropped in. It was always a pleasant surprise. And Joanna generally brought gifts, which made her an even more welcome guest than the usual.

"I made brownies!" Joanna called when she opened the car door.

Every time. Debbie laughed to herself. Joanna couldn't help it. She was a generous soul and never failed to shower her friends with her gifts and goodies.

"Brownies? You read my mind. I was desperate for something chocolate earlier today and thought I'd have to go to the shops. You're a lifesaver."

"I'm so glad. I'll put these in the kitchen and meet you in the garden if you like. I wore exactly the right clothes for gardening, since I was in my own garden earlier."

Debbie embraced her friend, then left her to return to the backyard. Joanna joined her before long, with a cap on her head and gloves she'd found in Debbie's small shed on her hands.

"I borrowed your gloves. I hope you don't mind."

"You're welcome to them," Debbie replied. "If you'll help me with this pumpkin vine. It's out of control."

"They always are," Joanna murmured as she surveyed the vine. "Happy to help."

As they worked, Debbie couldn't keep her gaze from drifting back over to the neighbours' house. She hadn't been able to stop thinking about what she'd seen.

"What are you looking at?" Joanna asked as she snipped a vine and tossed it over her shoulder into the pile that was forming behind her.

"My neighbours' house. I saw something the other day that bothered me."

"What was it?"

"Caleb reassures me it was nothing. But I saw the neighbour, Tim, pulling something heavy out of the house and putting it into his truck. He drove off in the direction of the state park."

"What was it?"

"I don't know. But it was wrapped in a blanket or some kind of fabric. And it was very heavy. It weighed the truck down when he put it inside."

"So? That could be anything. What are you thinking?" Joanna said.

"Well... where's his wife? He's married to a woman named Anna. I don't know her well, but I usually see her going to Pilates or walking on the beach. And since he made that trip, I haven't seen her. Not once."

Joanna shook her head with a smile. "That doesn't necessarily mean anything."

"I know it doesn't. But it is suspicious. Don't you think?"

"I don't know... maybe."

They finished trimming the pumpkin vine and moved on to weeding the vegetable patch.

"You probably shouldn't read too much into it," Joanna said. "I'm sure there's a perfectly reasonable explanation as to why you haven't seen Anna lately."

"You're right, of course. That's what Caleb says too. But I can't help worrying about her. Maybe I should go over there and confront him."

"Definitely not," Joanna said. "If he's done nothing wrong, you'll ruin your relationship with a neighbour, which is not something anyone should do if they want to live a peaceful life. And if he is a demented murderer, maybe he'll kill you. You should be a bit sneakier than that if you want to discover the truth."

"I already went over there and knocked on the door, but no one answered."

"Try again. You can take some of my brownies if you want. It'll be for a good cause." Joanna pulled on a carrot top, and an enormous carrot emerged from the dirt. "Wow, look at this!"

Debbie grinned. "That's the biggest one so far."

"You've become quite the domestic, Debbie Holmes," Joanna said with a wink. "Who would ever have thought?"

"I don't know who I'm becoming. Honestly, I don't recognise myself in the mirror anymore."

"It's a good thing, honey. This is a new season of life, and I'm really glad to see you embracing it with both arms."

"I hope I won't lose my mind in the process," Debbie quipped. "I forgot to ask you how your date went."

Joanna smiled as she reached for another carrot top. "Well, we had a lovely time." She grunted and pulled. A carrot burst through the dirt, and she brushed it off.

"That doesn't sound very exciting."

"It was, only... he didn't kiss me goodnight."

"Were you expecting him to?"

"I hoped he would. I don't know how I feel exactly. The whole thing is very disconcerting. We're friends and have been for a long time, but he's taken it to the next level by asking me for a date. So, I expected him to at least try for a kiss or ask to come in. He did neither, which makes me wonder if something went wrong and he changed his mind about me."

"You're overthinking things, which is exactly what I would do. But he's probably trying to take things slowly *because* you're lifelong friends. And that's a good thing. Don't rush it. You should both make sure it's right before you take that next step because once you do, there's no going back. Right?"

"Right. I've forgotten how all this works. I feel very rusty."

Joanna brushed a strand of hair away from her face and left a streak of dirt on her cheek.

Debbie removed a glove and reached out a hand to wipe her friend's cheek clean. "Don't worry so much. You're having a nice time. A man likes you and asked you on date. Enjoy it. Dating is the fun part."

"Yes, it is. Of course it is. I should forget about the pressure to be something more, or to act in a certain way. We're not teenagers."

"Thank goodness for that," Debbie said with a groan.

"Absolutely. Thanks, Deb. Good perspective shift. I'll let things unfold instead of trying to control them."

"It's more fun that way."

Chapter Sixteen

The next day, Beth stopped at a drive-through coffee shop and ordered a cappuccino. As she sat waiting for it to be delivered, she turned up the radio, hoping the music would give her a little more energy. She hadn't slept well the night before, tossing and turning until all hours. It was probably because she had a job interview today. Those always made her nervous.

The interview had gone well. She'd clicked with the interview panel and had given them extensive answers to their questions. They seemed interested in her as prospective employee, and from her experience in the past, she expected they would probably give her a call. But she wasn't entirely sure she wanted the job yet. It was back in Brisbane, in the city. And she'd left that life behind her not so long ago.

Of course, it was ridiculous to expect to find a graphic design job close to Sunshine, but she'd hoped she might. It would be like winning the lottery to have such specific criteria met. Still, she couldn't help hoping.

The attendant handed her the coffee, and she set it in her cup holder to drive out of the parking lot and back onto the street. She was in her old neighbourhood, and since she was going to be in town, she had booked herself for a hair appointment and to get her nails done. Why not? She hadn't had her hair done in weeks, and it was well overdue for highlights.

She pulled into the hairdresser's parking lot, then took a sip of coffee as she climbed out of the car. The other reason she wanted to get her hair and nails done was that Christmas was coming up. The whole family were headed to Sunshine to spend Christmas at Brandon's house. Mum wasn't thrilled about the prospect since she usually hosted, and Dad would be bringing his fiancée along, but she realised that her flat wasn't big enough to accommodate everyone.

New Year's Eve would be next. The thought of it set her stomach churning. She was putting herself into a situation where she was going to be hurt. The chances of Damien showing were slim. She'd been over it in her head a hundred times, and yet she continued planning for that evening as though he would be there. She was lining herself up for heartbreak.

The memory of that night still hung in her subconscious. She'd even dreamed about him a few nights earlier, that they were back on the Ferris wheel. There were bright lights all around. She was holding a half-eaten bag of pink and blue fairy floss. He had a Dagwood dog in one hand and some sauce on his chin.

They were talking and laughing. Everything he said was interesting or funny. Everything she said was witty and insightful. She'd never been so intriguing in all her life. Even she was amazed at the things she'd said. Now she couldn't recall exactly what they were, but she remembered the way he hung on every word and laughed at all her jokes as though she was the funniest girl in the world.

The hairdresser recognised her and waved her to a chair. She immediately launched into a story about a previous client that Beth only half listened to. Her thoughts were elsewhere, wandering over that New Year's Eve so many years earlier.

She saw Damien's brown eyes, sparkling beneath the colourful lights of the fireworks. He'd slipped his hand around hers and held it tight. His hand was hot, and she felt her pulse quicken at his touch. She'd never felt anything like it before. She'd had crushes, but nothing that was reciprocated. And nothing like this. From the first moment she saw him standing by the open-mouthed clowns with their heads moving back and forth, waiting for balls to be thrown into the gaping darkness, she'd been smitten.

Love at first sight. It was such a cliché. So very Romeo and Juliet of her, and she didn't even like that play. They'd studied it in English class the previous semester, and she'd gagged and laughed over their ridiculously over-the-top love for one another. Who fell for someone so quickly? It was unrealistic and soppy. But the moment her eyes landed on him, her heart had leapt into her throat, and she couldn't look away.

How had she known? One look, one glance, one moment of their eyes meeting, and something deep inside of her had a chemical reaction. Some part of her had known how well they'd connect. How much they'd have in common. Without one word being spoken.

He'd seen her, and his gaze was piercing. He hadn't taken his eyes off her from then on. He was with another boy who'd turned out to be his older brother, and they'd played almost every game at the festival. She and Jemma had followed at a distance, pretending not to notice them but keeping them in sight. She'd told Jemma, "I can't lose him. He's my soulmate —I just know it. I'm in love."

"I thought you didn't believe in love at first sight. Didn't you say it was sappy and unrealistic?" Jemma asked.

"I said that—it's true. But it's happened to me, and I can't deny it."

"You sound weird."

"Sorry, it's out of my control."

She was a good friend, though, and helped Beth keep a close eye on the two boys. They'd never seen them around before. Clearly they must've been from out of town. There were out-of-towners all over the island for the summer, and it hurt Beth to realise that meant they'd leave at some point. They were only there for a holiday. Maybe even for that day, and no more. Then she'd likely never see him again, and the pain of that would kill her. Or worse, she would live through it, never to feel this way about anyone ever again.

She could look back now and see how dramatic she'd been as a thirteen-year-old. But the poignant ache that she'd experienced then came back to her now and tore at her throat. He might not show up, but she had to be there. And if she was going to be there, she wanted to look her best.

"I'm going to book another appointment for New Year's," she said to the hairdresser.

"No worries, honey. I've got a spot that opened up this morning for the week after Christmas, and I'll reserve it just for you."

Chapter Seventeen

Gwen unpacked a Christmas wreath from a box of decorations she'd stowed at a storage facility just outside of town after she sold the family home. She tipped her head to one side to survey it. It was still beautiful, even after all these years. She'd made it herself a decade earlier and had hung it on her front door every year since. But now, she was living in a flat, and it didn't seem like the right fit any longer. It was perfect for the inn, though.

She walked to the inn's heavy front door, pulled it open, and hung the wreath. Then she shut it again and returned to the box to see what else she should hang. She'd hired a professional to do most of the Christmas decorations, but she wanted to add some of her own personal touches to give the place a homey feel.

There was a rocking horse that would go perfectly by the reception desk. And an angel for the top of the tree. She finished by setting a small china house by the front window and plugging it in so the little candle in the house glowed as though someone lived inside. The house was surrounded by snow, and there were two evergreens and a sleigh with children riding in it, that she set up beside the house.

With a sigh, she straightened her back and took it all in. The whole place looked delightful, ready for the holiday season. She smiled as she spun slowly on her heel. There were twinkle lights in the entryway, along with an enormous Christmas tree. There were wrapped gifts beneath the tree, and matching baubles dotting its green branches. Christmas music played softly through the sound system while the scent of cinnamon and chocolate wafted in from the restaurant. The inn was like a Christmas wonderland minus the snow and with stifling heat rushing in through the door every time it was opened.

This time, the door was opened by a man she didn't recognise. She strode to greet him and to make sure he shut the door before the air conditioning inside was overcome by the summer heatwave outside.

"Good morning," she said in a chipper voice. "Checking in?"

He took off his hat and crushed it between his hands, then looked around as though searching for something or someone. "Hi. No, not checking in."

His accent was soft and familiar. His thick black hair had streaks of grey. His weathered face was handsome and his forearms were thick and muscular, as though he'd worked hard throughout his life.

"Can I help you?" Gwen asked.

"Yes, I'm looking for Fran."

"Francesca?"

"That's right," he said.

"I'll find her for you. Can I tell her what this is about?"

"Certainly," he said, his voice smooth and deep. He had a moustache, and his brown eyes were kind. "My name is Alberto. I'm an old friend."

Gwen hurried to find her concierge. All the while, her mind raced. Francesca didn't have family in Australia, and she hadn't mentioned any friends, either. Who was this man? Why was he here? She was dying to find out more.

Francesca was in the dining room helping some guests with directions. Gwen waited until she was free, then pulled her to one side.

"There's a man waiting for you in reception. He says he's an old friend of yours—Alberto."

Francesca's face paled. "Alberto?"

"That's right. Do you want to see him? I can send him away..."

Francesca steadied herself with one hand against the wall. "No, it's fine. I haven't seen him in many years. I wonder why he is here."

"Does he live in Australia?"

She shook her head. "Last I heard, he was in Milan. He's in the fashion industry."

"Oh?" Gwen wanted to know more but didn't want to pry.

"Thank you," Fran said, before heading in the direction of the reception counter.

Gwen followed at a distance. She peeped around the wall just as Fran found Alberto, and watched as Fran greeted him. She was serene, her voice so quiet that Gwen couldn't hear what she said. Then Alberto grabbed her with both hands, one on each arm. Gwen gasped. Would he harm her? Her heart skipped a beat. Then she breathed a sigh of relief as the man embraced Fran.

Gwen pressed a hand to her chest as her heart rate returned to normal. Gradually, Fran raised her arms to encircle Albert's waist in a hug. Gwen pretended to be tidying the reception desk while studying the two of them out of the corner of her eye. Alberto was a mystery. And from the look on Fran's face when Gwen told her he was there, Gwen was certain there was more to their relationship than either of them had let on. But what she didn't know yet was whether their past was one of affection or conflict. Was he an enemy, or a friend? She couldn't say.

Just then, there was an enormous crash in the kitchen. Gwen's adrenaline spiked again as she rushed through the dining room to find out what had happened. Her anxiety levels had been rising ever since she opened the inn, and it didn't take much for her to leap directly into a state of panic these days. She discovered a staff member with a pile of broken, dirty plates at her feet, a look of dismay on her pretty face.

Gwen patted her arm. "Never mind. They're only plates." She drew a deep breath to calm her nerves, grateful it hadn't been worse.

Chapter Eighteen

It'd been a week since Chris and Joanna had been on their date. Joanna was beginning to wonder if she'd ever see him again when he popped into her garden that Friday afternoon. She was on her knees, working on a particularly stubborn weed, when he ambled across the grass with a smile on his handsome face, his grey hair riffled by a cool sea breeze.

Joanna stopped working and wiped a bead of sweat from her brow with the back of her arm as she watched him approach. She offered him a wide smile.

"Fancy seeing you here."

"I thought I might find you hunched over your garden bed. It's your usual afternoon haunt." He chuckled. "I've been doing much the same for the past hour, although I'm ready to have a break."

She wanted to ask why he hadn't called or visited since their date, but she hated to draw attention to the awkwardness she felt between them. Instead, she preferred to pretend that there was nothing amiss. And maybe she was overreacting, anyway. She'd never been much good at this kind of thing, even when she'd dated her husband all those years ago.

He sat on a garden bench she'd had installed about five years earlier. It was a beautiful timber piece and complemented the flower bed behind it nicely.

"How's your week been?"

She stood stiffly to her feet and straightened her legs with a groan. "It takes longer and longer to get up from the ground these days."

"I know exactly what you mean."

"My week has been fine. I've been thinking about my new cookbook. I'm going to focus on events for a series, actually. My editor is on board. I thought I might start with Christmas, since that's coming up soon."

"I like the idea."

"Then I'll do weddings, birthdays and so on. It'll be a whole thing."

He laughed. "Sounds like a winner to me."

"Speaking of which," she continued. "We're doing a Christmas special for our potluck brunch. Would you like to come? We're inviting family and friends to join us."

"I'd love that," he said. "Just let me know when and what to bring, and I'll be there."

"I think I'm going to ask everyone to bring their favourite Christmas family recipe. The dish that reminds you it's Christmastime. For me, that was always potato salad. A recipe passed down through the family for generations. And Gwen has a roast pork recipe that everyone loves. She's going to spoil us with that."

"I know exactly what to bring," Chris replied. "My grandmother used to make a killer stuffing mix that she'd use to stuff the turkey at Christmas time, and I have the recipe."

"Perfect. We don't have anyone bringing stuffing yet."

"And gravy too, if you don't mind. I love to make my world-famous gravy."

"World famous?" She quirked an eyebrow.

"Haven't you heard about it?" he quipped.

She laughed. "Now that you mention it... there was a report of a man in Sunshine who took the world by storm with his delicious gravy recipe. I recall a news helicopter hovering overhead, and a bevy of reporters were searching for him earlier today."

He grinned. "Don't spill my secret."

* * *

Chris asked if she'd like to take a walk on the beach with him when she finished gardening. So she changed clothes and donned a hat and met him outside. They left their sandals at the beach entrance beside a tuft of seagrass.

"I meant to tell you earlier that I'm going to spend Christmas Eve and Christmas Day with my family down in Sydney," he said as they stepped onto the beach.

Joanna's toes dug into the soft sand. She pushed forward, startling a seagull that flapped out of her way with a squawk. "That should be nice."

"I wasn't sure if we're at that stage... where we tell each other our plans. So, I decided I'd tell you, and then you could choose whether or not the topic is of interest."

She glanced over at him and saw that he was watching her, eyes sparkling. She laughed. "Oh, well, I'm not sure about that either. But thanks for letting me know. I was curious."

"Good. I'm glad. What will you be doing for Christmas?"

"I'll be here, with Eva and the baby. And I've invited Aaron and Emily over as well, and Wanda, Emily's sister, with her two children. So, I'm going to have a pretty full house."

"That sounds good," he replied. "I wish I could be here. But I'm looking forward to seeing my son and his family. I haven't been down to visit them in Sydney over the past few months, and I miss them."

"I know you'll have a lovely time."

Did he regret their date? Or did he want to see her again? She didn't want to push. Maybe she was old-fashioned that way. But if he had enjoyed their date, he would ask her out again. There was no point in her making an issue of it. If he didn't want to ask her out again, he wouldn't. And she'd rather not hear him say those words. It might impact their friendship.

She dipped her head to look at the sand as they walked. Even though it was outdoors in the elements, with animals and birds, humans and waves impacting it every single day, it was fresh and clean. Warm around her bare feet, it felt comforting against her skin. She loved the beach so much. It'd become a part of her. Who she was. She couldn't imagine living anywhere else.

She'd spent a lifetime beside the shores of the ocean, and it filled her soul with a peace she couldn't understand but was grateful for all the same. She'd spent years looking at the beach from a distance, too afraid to step out into the open but longing to push her toes into the warm sand. And for a moment, she revelled in the fact that she was there, experiencing that very longed-for feeling, with a very good friend by her side.

Chapter Nineteen

It was a hot day. So hot that Debbie had spent much of the morning either in the pool or padding about in the air-conditioning inside the beach house. She hadn't tried to venture out, even though she did most days, because the air was humid and clung to her body like a warm, wet glove the moment she stepped outside. There was a chaise lounge by the window that looked out over her swimming pool and into the neighbours' yard, and she carried a cup of tea and a book over to the lounge to read.

Isn't this what retired people are supposed to do?

She sighed as she sat, then rested her legs on the lounge. She opened the book and let it sit on her chest, pages apart. Her anxiety levels had been high all week, and she didn't know why. She should've been relaxed and content. She'd been retired now for months. And yet, she was still living on edge, as though she expected to commute to the city to try a case in court at any moment.

The neighbours' garage door was shut, and she'd seen Anna leave about an hour earlier. She was dressed in pilates gear, so she was likely headed to the gym. Obviously, Debbie had been wrong about Tim killing her. She was very much alive. She was relieved to have her fears turn out to be unfounded, although she was still convinced that Tim was up to something.

Ever since that day, she'd seen him sneaking around the outside of the house, stashing things in the garden shed and locking it. She'd tried to peer in through the windows to see if she could spy anything, but the windows were too dirty. She should take cleaning supplies with her next time. Caleb had suggested she was losing her mind and shouldn't be so nosy. She didn't want to prove him right.

She took a sip of tea, then sat up as a young woman scurried down the neighbours' drive and slipped into the house through a side door.

Debbie's heart skipped a beat. Who was that? She hadn't recognised her. And why was she going into the house when Anna was clearly out? It was suspicious. She'd known he was hiding something. Maybe that something was a mistress. Perhaps he'd been stashing things in the garden shed to do with an affair—things he didn't want Anna to see.

She got to her feet and hurried across the living room, then out through the front door and across into the neighbours' yard. She moved quickly and quietly, on her toes. Her leggings were too hot in this weather, but she didn't plan to be outside for long. She intended to confront Tim, tell him she knew what he was doing, and then spin on her heel and march back to her house with the comfort of knowing she'd stopped him from doing anything worse than he'd already done.

Her pulse increased the closer she got to the front door, and sweat beaded on her forehead as she raised her fist to knock. Then she hesitated—if she knocked, they'd stop whatever they were doing. She needed to catch them in the act to be sure. She lowered her hand to the doorknob, turned it, and pushed the door open.

People leapt out from behind furniture from every direction at once and yelled, "Surprise!" Debbie's heart jumped into her throat, beating a hundred miles per hour.

"What on earth?"

Tim raised both hands and walked towards her. "Sorry, Debbie. We didn't realise it was you. It's okay, everyone. This is my neighbour."

There were sighs and exclamations of disappointment as the group milled about and quietly got back into place.

Debbie grimaced. "I'm so sorry, Tim. I'm interrupting."

"No, it's fine. But come and hide with us, since we're expecting Anna at any moment."

Debbie hurried to get behind an armchair, ducking down low next to Tim.

"It's her birthday," he explained in a whisper.

Debbie's cheeks flushed with warmth as embarrassment swamped her. She'd gotten it wrong again. Tim wasn't having an affair. If she was going to snoop, perhaps she should've paid a little more attention rather than jumping to conclusions. This time her conclusion was spectacularly off the mark. She could imagine what Caleb's face would look like when she told him what she'd done.

A car pulled up the driveway, and a door slammed. When Anna walked inside, the group jumped out again and shouted "Surprise!" This time Debbie joined them.

Anna gaped, then quickly fell into broad smiles as people greeted her one by one.

Debbie wished Anna a happy birthday and told Tim thank you and sorry again. Then she hurried back to her house, shame burning in her chest.

She stood in the kitchen, sipping her reheated tea, staring at the wall. This was no good. She needed something to occupy her time, to keep her mind from wandering. She wanted to do something creative. Something that would contribute to the world.

It was time to write that book she'd always dreamed of writing. With a smile on her face, she made her way to the office and sat in front of her computer. Then she began to type.

Chapter Twenty

That summer had been a hard one for Beth. She was remembering what it had been like — thirteen years old, and school was done for the year. She and Jemma had been bored with nothing to do for a full three weeks. She'd begged her parents to take a trip, to go somewhere and do something interesting. So many of her school friends were driving to visit relatives or flying overseas for a holiday. One friend was going with her family to Japan for a ski trip. Beth was jealous. Usually it was her family jetting off somewhere to get away from Sunshine. But not this year.

This year, her mother had decided to renovate the house. Her parents were fighting all the time. Did they want the brown paint or the blue? The oversized armchair, or the twin armchairs? The big tiles or the small in the bathroom? It was noisy and annoying. And all she wanted to do was get out of there.

She ran down the footpath beside Sunshine Beach, scanning all the while to see if Jemma was already there. She spotted her down by the water's edge with a group of kids and changed course to intercept her before she plunged into the water. Jemma wore a red triangle bikini, and her skin was deeply tanned after weeks of swimming and lying in the sun.

"Jemma!" she called.

Beth's feet burned in the sand, and she scuttled with puckered lips to the water's edge.

Jemma faced her with a grin and came to meet her. "I was wondering when you'd get here. You took long enough."

"Mum made me wash the walls with something called sugar soap. I told her, if she's poisoning me with that stuff, I'm going to come back and haunt her."

Jemma laughed. "It's just soap."

"Well, I'm never washing walls again. I don't see the point. The walls are always clean, and I told her that. She said, that's because she washes them regularly and that it's about time I contribute. As if I don't do the dishes every day. She never sees the hard work I do."

Jemma shrugged. "I don't know. I like your mum. She's always nice to me. And she makes the best choc-chip cookies."

"That's true," Beth said. All the kids knew her mother made the best baked goods. They loved visiting Beth's house. And usually they'd spend the summer there, swimming in the pool and eating. But this year, the renovation was ruining Beth's life. She couldn't wait for it to be over.

Beth threw her white cotton dress onto the pile of towels the others had dumped. Then she and Jemma ran into the surf with shouts over the cold water. They swam for around an hour, bodysurfing the waves to shore and then trudging back out again. By the time they were finished, Beth's eyes were stinging, and she regretted not putting suncream on her shoulders.

"I think I'm burned," she said, pressing her fingertips to the hot skin on her arms.

"You're so tanned, you won't be able to tell," Jemma replied as she towelled herself dry.

"Let's stop and get some aloe in town."

"I really want to get a cream bun. I'm dying of hunger."

They loved to stop by the bakery. There was a fish-and-chip shop next to it, and they usually bought something at one or the other. Sometimes both. Beth was ravenous all the time and couldn't seem to slow down her eating. She couldn't remember a time when she'd been as hungry as she was this summer, and she'd grown at least ten centimetres in the past six months. She might even end up taller than her mother, something she'd never thought would happen since she'd always been the tiny one in her group of friends. But now she was the same height as Jemma and might even be slightly taller, a possibility she loved to tease her friend over.

As they walked to the bakery, Beth's thoughts turned to the festival that night. It was New Year's Eve, and they'd decided they would go to the celebration on Sunshine Beach together.

"So, we're meeting at seven. Right?"

"That's right. My parents want to have a family dinner before the festival. Otherwise, we could meet up earlier."

"Mine too," Beth lied. She didn't know what her family was planning because all her parents did was yell at each other. She hoped they weren't going to get a divorce. There was a girl at school called Jodie whose parents had divorced the previous year, and she'd ended up moving away to the city. They didn't hear from her again, even though she'd promised she write and call every day. But Beth didn't want to think about that happening to her family. Her parents loved each other—she was certain of that. They just shouldn't be involved in renovations. That was the real issue.

Dad had a lot of opinions, and a bad temper. Mum liked to be in control, so they simply didn't get along when they were working on a project together. Usually, they did things separately, and that worked out fine.

The cream buns from the bakery were sticky and soft. The centre was piped full of firm, sweet cream, and the combination was divine. They sat on a bench outside the bakery to watch the world go by as they ate. Beth got cream all over her mouth and chin, but it was worth it. She licked herself clean, then used a napkin to get the rest of it. Jemma was a slow eater and took her time. Finally, she was finished, and they continued walking down the street and into the main part of the small town.

"What should we do now?" Jemma asked.

"I want to get out of the sun."

"We could go to your house and lay in the shade by the pool."

"My parents are at each other's throats. Dad's taken some time off to help Mum with the reno and for Christmas and the New Year. It's a disaster."

"How about my place, then?"

Beth didn't like going to Jemma's. They lived in a tiny house in the most built-up part of town, and her brothers liked nothing more than to harass whoever Jemma brought over.

"We could go to the library."

"They won't like us sitting on the chairs while we're still wet."

"That's true," Beth admitted. "Okay, fine. We can go to my place. But we might need to get ear plugs first."

Jemma laughed. "It can't be that bad."

"Trust me."

At the house, Brandon was in the driveway working on his bomb of a car. He was so proud of that thing. He'd bought it with the money he'd earned working part time at a restaurant while he studied law. He lived in Brisbane now, and he only came home on weekends and holidays. As much of a pain as he sometimes acted, Beth had to admit that she missed having him in the house all the time. He'd been good about taking her places and was easy to talk to. It was nice to have him home.

"Going for a swim?" he asked as he wiped grease off his hands with a rag.

Jemma smiled shyly at him. She'd always had a crush on Brandon, and he knew it. He smiled back so that his dimples showed.

"Maybe," Beth replied. "Hey, have they stopped yelling yet?"

Brandon laughed. "Yeah, Dad went out half an hour ago. Said he had to get out of this house, since it was suffocating him."

"I'm so sick of the fighting."

"Me too, but there's chocolate mud cake. So, that kind of makes up for it." Brandon winked at Jemma as the two girls walked away, and Beth noticed that her cheeks looked awfully red.

"I don't know if I can eat cake after that bun," Beth said.

Jemma didn't respond. Instead, she glanced back at Brandon, who had returned his attention to the car. "How long will your brother be home?"

"Until February, I think."

"Hmmm."

"Don't even..."

"What?" Jemma blinked. "I didn't. I wouldn't."

"You had better not. He's my brother. Ewww."

"He's cute," Jemma replied with a shrug.

"He's gross. You have no idea. This morning, I saw him fart on Hilton. Right on his leg."

Jemma giggled. "No, he didn't."

"I swear, he did. And then they rolled around on the

ground for like ten minutes, punching each other in the arm. They're juvenile."

Jemma pushed open the front door. "Still, he's cute. And he has a car."

"He might be cute, but ewww."

"You do realise that all the girls in Sunshine disagree with you."

They padded through the living room. The smell of chocolate cake drew them into the kitchen. Beth realised she could probably eat one slice. Definitely no more than that, though.

"There's a decided lack of cute boys in our town. I've got to get out of here," she said.

Jemma nodded as Beth sliced them each a piece of cake and placed them on napkins. "I know what you mean. We've grown up with every single one of the boys our age."

"I can't imagine dating any of them. How are we supposed to find a boyfriend one day?" Beth wrinkled her nose and handed Jemma a napkin-wrapped piece of cake.

They walked out the back door to the pool and dropped onto banana lounges side by side.

"I have no idea. Maybe we'll have to wait until we leave the island to find dates."

"That's a depressing thought." Beth took a bite of cake. Suddenly, she was hungry.

* * *

That night, Beth's shoulders tingled from the sunburn. She'd added aloe to them three times over the course of the afternoon, but she could tell they would be very red the next day. So, she wore a light dress to the festival, with thin straps that barely touched her skin.

Beside her, Jemma was slamming a giant hammer down

on a target to see if she could beat the record. But Beth wasn't interested in that game. She wanted to go on the dodgem cars. They were her favourite. She glanced around the festival while she waited. There were a lot of familiar faces, but more tourists than locals.

The New Year's Eve festival on Sunshine Beach was something people came from all over the southeast to attend. Watching the midnight fireworks light up the sky above the rolling waves had become something of a tradition. The town's quaint beauty drew people from miles around who wanted to get away from the city for a little while for some peace and quiet. The irony was, they brought the bustle and noise with them. But Beth didn't mind. She liked it when the sleepy town came awake over the summer, its size swelling to more than double what it usually was.

"Anyone interesting here?" Jemma asked when she finally finished the game.

"I don't know. Let's go for a walk."

They wandered down the footpath beside the beach. Beth wore a pair of strappy sandals, and her long legs were tanned and lithe from all the running she'd done in recent months. She'd joined the running club with her mother. Mum said it was something they could do together, bond over. Beth didn't mind. She quite liked running and had even been part of the school's cross-country team at the districts earlier in the year.

Then she saw a boy standing near the lemonade stand. He was alone—at least it looked as though he was. When she spied him, he had his hands in his pockets. The wind lifted his dark blond hair and made it stand on end briefly. Then it flopped back down on his forehead. As she looked at him, her breath caught in her throat.

"Who is that?" she whispered.

"Huh?" Jemma stopped walking. "Where?"

"Over there. Don't look!" Beth's cheeks burned as Jemma searched the crowd.

"Oh, the guy by the lemonade table?"

Beth nodded and turned away. "Don't stare at him. Oh, my goodness. He's perfect."

Jemma grinned. "He's pretty hot, I'll admit. So, you should go and talk to him."

The boy looked to be about fifteen. He was taller than Beth and Jemma, and there was another boy with him who was older still. They looked similar. Maybe they were brothers.

"I can't just go up and talk to him. I don't know him."

"Of course you can. Ask him for directions or something."

Beth frowned. "I live here. I don't need directions."

Jemma grunted. "It's just an excuse, silly."

"I'll need something better than that. He's an out-of-towner, and I'm not."

"Fine. Ask him about the lemonade."

"That's lame." Beth glanced back at the boy, worried he would leave while she was busy bickering with Jemma over lemonade-related questions.

"Fine. Come up with your own questions, then."

Just then, the boy turned and made eye contact with Beth. Her heart skipped a beat. His lips turned up into a smile. She felt as though the earth shook beneath her feet. Or at least, that it should. That's how great that smile was.

"Wow, you're so lucky. The boys you like always like you back." Jemma flipped her hair over her shoulder with one hand. "I really should hate you."

"But you can't hate me. I'm your best friend."

"That, and you're too adorable." Jemma sighed. "Go over there."

This time, Beth didn't object. The boy was still staring at her. He hadn't moved. So she stumbled in his direction, feeling as though the earth was spinning a little faster than it usually did.

"Hi," he said.

"Hi."

Jemma nudged her with an elbow.

"Do you like the lemonade?" Beth asked.

His brow furrowed. "Huh? Oh, I haven't had any."

"I'm Beth," she said.

His smile widened. "I'm Damien."

Chapter Twenty-One

"I thought we were using the blue mugs with the coffee service tonight," the waitress said, her brow furrowed.

Gwen adopted her most patient tone. "No, those cups are for the inn, to be used for room service and in the dining room. The white mugs are for the restaurant."

"Oh, right. Got it. I think..." The girl shook her head slowly, her brown ponytail waving back and forth. "It's so complicated."

Gwen smiled. "I suppose that's true. There's a lot to remember. But you're doing a great job."

"Thanks."

The girl wandered off in the wrong direction, away from the restaurant and back into the inn. Gwen sighed. Finding and training new staff was harder than she'd ever imagined it would be. But at least she had Fran on her side now, and Fran was so good with the staff. She never seemed to lose her cool, either. She was always level-headed, patient and calm, no matter what. Gwen had already learned a lot from her about how to manage the team.

Speaking of which, she needed to go after the girl and

bring her back since she was on table service in the restaurant starting in ten minutes. And who knew where she was headed now? Did she think she was working inside the inn? Another sigh, and Gwen set down the stack of menus she'd been wiping clean.

She found the girl in the dining room, stacking blue mugs as if to take them somewhere.

"What are you doing with those mugs?" she asked in as sweet a voice as she could manage given the circumstances.

"I'm taking them into the restaurant."

Gwen offered her a smile. "Oh, wow, that's so thoughtful. But let's leave them here because we're using the white mugs in the restaurant. Blue is for the inn. White for the restaurant. Okay?"

"White. Gotcha." The girl grinned, then trotted back to the restaurant.

"These kids will be the death of me," Gwen muttered beneath her breath.

Just then, she heard raised voices in the reception area. She hurried out to see what was going on, her heart in her throat. They hadn't experienced any kind of violent altercations with guests yet, and she hoped they would avoid that today as well. It was the last thing she needed after a long day on her feet.

But there were no guests waiting in reception other than the Italian man who'd come the previous day to visit Fran. The two of them were huddled in the sitting area off to one side, whisper-shouting at one another. Then the man raised his voice.

"You can't just ignore me, Fran."

"Hush," Fran replied with a glance in Gwen's direction. "This is my workplace."

He reached out to grab hold of both of her arms. "Please listen to me. I'm begging you."

Fran shook off his grasp. "I don't want to hear what you have to say. You've got to leave. I'm working."

She strode from the room, her face full of sorrow. Gwen watched her go, surprised to witness the level of emotion between the two of them. What was going on? Why was Fran so upset? And why wouldn't she listen to this man? Gwen still didn't know anything about him. Fran hadn't wanted to say a thing when she'd asked a few probing questions and Gwen hated to push her, especially after everything she'd been through recently. But now that their situation was beginning to disrupt her work, Gwen would have to find out why this man had come to the inn to see Fran.

She was about to follow Fran out to the back deck, but the man pushed past her. Gwen frowned, then followed both of them. Fran had hurried through the kitchen and out the back door, where the staff were setting up for the evening meal on the deck. Fairy lights twinkled. Soft music issued from the speakers. Several of the guests sat at the bar, sipping drinks.

Fran had stopped at the bar and was speaking to one of the bar staff. She saw the man approaching and stepped out from behind the bar to leave, but he blocked her path and spoke to her in Italian.

She shook her head. "English, please."

"Fran, I need to speak with you," he replied.

Gwen wondered if she should intervene.

"It won't change anything," Fran said with a sigh of resignation.

"But I love you."

Gwen gasped quietly. She set a table with clean glasses while she listened.

"Alberto, you can't say that," Fran replied gently.

"I've always loved you, and you know that. When you moved away, it broke my heart."

"You married and had a family. You were happy." It

sounded as though Fran was trying to convince herself, willing it to be true.

"I had a life of joy, but without you. And now that my wife is gone and your husband too, we can finally be together. I flew here to tell you that. I wanted you to know after all this time."

Fran shook her head. "No, my heart is empty. I have nothing left to give anyone."

"You're grieving. I will wait." He reached out to hold her hand.

She shook it free. "I can't. I'm sorry, Alberto." She scurried past Gwen and back into the inn.

Alberto stood alone, dejected. His arms hung by his sides, and he stared at the doorway where Fran had disappeared. Gwen added silverware to the table, her heart pounding. She felt sorry for Alberto. He'd poured out his heart to Fran, and she'd rejected him. But she was still in mourning for her husband. Surely he knew that. He had to give her some time.

She offered him a weak smile as he strode past her and through the door. She followed and watched him leave. Her new concierge had certainly brought a measure of intrigue to the inn. Gwen could hardly wait to find out what would happen next.

Chapter Twenty-Two

Joanna yawned as she pulled her car into the inn's parking lot. She hadn't been getting much sleep lately. Her great-grand-daughter was teething and was waking up several times a night. At ten months of age, hopefully this phase wouldn't last long. Gypsy had become a decent sleeper when she was around three months old, then reverted to waking constantly at four months. Back to sleeping well again by six months, and now at ten months was waking again. Despite all of that, having Gypsy Rose at the house had already been such a breath of fresh air for her. She felt happier than she had in a long time, even if she couldn't stop yawning.

She parked the car and climbed out, looking across at the inn and restaurant for a moment before walking through the parking lot. Gwen had done such a wonderful job rehabili-tating the place. She was very proud of her friend, and she knew how hard she worked. Joanna was grateful not to have to work at the same pace, although Gwen seemed to thrive from it.

The inn was busy. Joanna entered through a side door near the library. There were several people in the space, reading.

The hallway was empty, but reception was filled with people checking into their rooms. She made her way through the dining area to the door that led to the restaurant, then marked off her checklist.

She'd visited the inn once per week since the initial opening to check that the staff were doing what they were supposed to do, that the kitchen was running the way it should. She'd put procedures in place to ensure everything was up to code and met her own standard. And so far, she'd only had to pull them up on one or two things. They were doing well, and she was pleased with how the restaurant was tracking.

Afterwards, she found Gwen upstairs in the large, walk-in linen closet. She shut the door behind her and got to work helping with the stocktake.

"You don't have to do that," Gwen said with a grateful smile.

"I enjoy it," Joanna replied. "Besides, you may never get finished if you try to do this yourself."

"I like the change of pace. It gives me a break from the craziness downstairs."

"I saw... you've got quite the crowd checking in."

"We're fully booked for the whole weekend."

"Your business is growing at a very satisfying rate," Joanna replied. "Congratulations."

"Thank you. I can hardly believe it. I thought it would take a lot longer for us to find traction. But Beth's been helping me do some social media marketing with the new branding she's put together, and it's making a big difference to bookings."

"How wonderful. You're very lucky to have her on board."

"Don't I know it," Gwen replied. "It won't be forever, but I'm taking advantage of having her here while I can."

"How is she? Is she looking for work?"

"She's applied for a few jobs and has interviews lined up, but I don't know if her heart is in it. She's enjoying having some time back in Sunshine, I think."

Joanna noted down the number of towels in the stack nearest, and began on the next. Gwen pushed a pen behind her ear, standing on tip-toe to reach a higher shelf. She pulled down an armful of towels in disarray, and folded them neatly. Then set them in a stack on a lower shelf and leaned forwards. "I don't know if I should say anything, but there's been a development with my concierge."

"Francesca? The woman whose husband died?" Joanna asked as she pulled out a step stool and sat on it to listen.

Gwen nodded.

"Well, I don't really know her, so if you don't feel comfortable telling me..."

Gwen hesitated. "I don't know who else to talk to, and it's eating me up."

"We can't have that. Go ahead then, for goodness' sake."

Gwen smiled. "I hoped you'd say that. Apparently, she has a stalker."

"What?" Joanna was alarmed. This wasn't good news. The poor woman might be in danger.

"Nothing bad—at least, I don't think so. He keeps coming to the inn to see her, and she doesn't seem to want to meet with him. I was worried, but then I overheard him say he loves her, that he always has, and that he couldn't hold it in any longer and flew here from Italy to tell her that."

"How sweet."

"I thought so too," Gwen said. "But Fran seems very upset that he's here. She said something about not having anything to give, and rushed off. I'm not sure if she's upset because of his timing..."

"It certainly could've been better," Joanna agreed. "Her husband has only been gone for a month or so."

"I think it's been six weeks."

"Hardly any time at all," Joanna replied.

Gwen shrugged. "I suppose they're not getting any younger. Perhaps he's trying to seize the day."

"Good point. It's hard to take sides here, really. I generally take the side of love. But then I also understand that Fran must be feeling very overwhelmed by it all. Or maybe she doesn't return his feelings."

"That's what I'm wondering," Gwen said with a sigh.

After they'd finished folding linens, they checked on the staff. Joanna walked Gwen through some of her suggestions for the restaurant, and then she drove her home. It was quiet in the car, each of them lost in their own thoughts. Finally, Gwen spoke.

"How are things with Chris?"

Joanna didn't know how to respond. She'd been trying not to think about it. "He's acting as though we didn't go on a date."

"Did something happen on the date?"

Joanna shrugged as she pulled up to the curb next to Gwen's apartment complex. "I don't know. At the time, I thought it was lovely, and he doesn't seem upset. We've gotten together a few times since. He comes over, as he always did, to spend time with me. We watch TV shows together, play Scrabble, laugh and have a great time."

"So, what's the problem, then?" Gwen asked.

Joanna sighed. "I sound like a silly teenaged schoolgirl all over again. The problem is, he hasn't kissed me yet."

Gwen laughed. "Oh, dear. That *is* a problem."

"Are you planning on going on a date anytime soon? Because it's not something I'm used to. I'm not sure how to behave, what to say, what to expect. It's all very confusing."

"Me?" Gwen asked incredulously. "Definitely not. I'm not

sure I'll ever go on a date again in my life. I'm very happy with the way things are now, and I have no plans to change that."

"You never know." Joanna replied. "I thought that too. And now I'm mooning about whether or not my neighbour likes me and when he'll kiss me."

They both broke into laughter.

Gwen patted Joanna on the arm. "Never mind. I'm sure if you pass me a note during maths class, and I pass the note to Chris, we can work this thing out between you two crazy kids."

Chapter Twenty-Three

Debbie glanced at the kitchen clock. She was running out of time. Everyone would be there for the BBQ soon, and Caleb still wasn't home from the city. He'd promised to come home early from work to help her set up the BBQ, but he wasn't there yet, and she hadn't had time to call him. She hated that they had to live separately for some of each week now and had decided she'd move back to the flat in the city during the week while he was at work, since she missed him so much.

But for now, they would have the weekend at the beach house together, and she couldn't wait to see him. There were butterflies in her stomach thinking about it. And as she slathered garlic butter on Turkish bread, she couldn't help smiling over that—they'd been married for decades, and she was still excited at the prospect of him walking through the door.

It wasn't always like that for them. But over the past year, they'd worked hard to rebuild their relationship, to bring back the romance and to focus on one another rather than their work. It'd been difficult at times, especially when her business was falling apart and required more than the usual attention.

But she was proud of how well they'd managed, and that their marriage was doing better than ever. At least, she thought it was. She'd have to ask Caleb if he felt the same way, although she was a little anxious to find out.

The garage door whirred up, and her butterflies buzzed frantically around in her gut. She poured two glasses of Pinot Noir and walked to the garage to hand Caleb a glass as he stepped inside.

"Wow, that's service," he said, bending to kiss her.

He took the glass in one hand and carried his briefcase with the other to the bedroom to change.

"Did you have a nice day?"

"It was fine. I told them I'd be pulling back on my hours soon."

"You did?"

He stepped out of the closet in a white shirt and boxers to grin at her.

"Why did you do that?"

"I want to spend more time together. I know it's been hard on you, losing your business the way you did. And now that you have all this spare time, I want to be here. We've always longed to travel—maybe if I can slow down, we can do some of that. We've got enough saved for retirement. More than enough, really, and I'm losing interest in the corporate grind. As you said, Matthew is very capable and ready to take over just as soon as I give him the nod."

"Your nephew is a miniature version of you."

He laughed at that. "I suppose you're right. He *is* a lot like me, although he looks like his mother."

"So, what did Matthew say?"

"He said he understood, and that he was excited to step up into my shoes when the time comes."

"Into your shoes? He said that?"

"He did. I told him, 'Whoa there, calm yourself, I'm not

leaving yet. You'll still have a little while before the shoes need filling.'"

Debbie sipped her wine. "I'm so glad, though. I'll be grateful to have you around more often. And I'm dying to do some travelling, but I didn't want to go without you."

"Maybe you should see if your friends want to take a trip with you. I won't be able to step away completely for a few more years yet, but I'll definitely try to take some time off now and then. And I'm going to cut back my hours—no more late nights. They will just have to cope without me."

"Gwen has taken on this whole inn project, and I doubt she'll be going anywhere for a while. But I'll ask Joanna about it."

The friends soon arrived. Joanna brought Chris with her, and Debbie was glad to see the two of them talking and laughing together, closer than they'd been. She knew Joanna was confused about where the relationship was headed, but to Debbie, it certainly looked as though Chris cared deeply for her friend. Gwen came alone, and was on the phone with Beth when she arrived.

Debbie welcomed them each with freshly made mojitos, and they sat outside next to the pool while Caleb and Chris chatted by the BBQ. Caleb was grilling prawns, scallops and pieces of fish to go with the fresh salads Debbie had made.

"What a lovely evening," Joanna said. "I'm glad that the sun is going down. It's been far too hot for my liking."

"I always forget why I love living in Sunshine until the winter months arrive," Gwen said as she swatted away a fly. "You can't beat a winter in Sunshine."

"That's very true," Debbie agreed.

"What have you been up to this week?" Joanna asked.

Debbie hesitated. She wanted to tell her friends about the confusion over her neighbours' surprise party, but she knew how bad it made her look. "You know I've been a bit nosy regarding my neighbours."

Joanna laughed. "That's right—you thought he was a serial killer for a while, didn't you? I hope you've given up on that one."

"Unfortunately, I took it a bit too far."

"What happened?" Gwen leaned forward.

Debbie cleared her throat. "I happened to see a woman sneak into the house when I knew for a fact that Anna was out —I'd seen her leave for her weekly pilates class earlier."

"Oh, no..." Joanna said, lifting a hand to her chest.

Debbie nodded. "Oh, yes... I went over there to confront him. And it turns out he was throwing a surprise party for his wife. They thought I was her, and they all leapt out and shouted 'surprise' at me. I just about had a heart attack."

Joanna and Gwen burst into gales of laughter. They laughed so hard that they had to wipe tears from their eyes before they were done. Debbie laughed with them.

"Okay, get it out of your system," she said with a chuckle. "I know, it's ridiculous."

"I can't believe you did that."

"Was your neighbour upset with you?"

"No, he was very kind. He asked me to stay and included me in the party."

"What a lovely man. Doesn't sound like a murderer at all." Joanna took another sip of mojito.

Debbie giggled. "Yes, and I learned my lesson."

"Did you, though?" Gwen asked.

"Yes, I did. I'm not going to be nosy any longer."

"I suppose we'll see..." Joanna didn't sound convinced.

"And I've started writing a book."

"Really? What kind of book?" Gwen asked.

"It's a fiction book about a woman who is married and struggling with infertility."

"Is it about your experiences?" Joanna asked in a gentle tone.

Debbie shook her head. "Not exactly. I'm going to draw on my personal journey, of course. But it's a fictional situation."

"I think that's fantastic," Joanna replied. "It'll be a great form of therapy. And I've always thought you should write. You have a wonderful way with words."

"Thank you," Debbie replied, feeling chuffed. "I appreciate the encouragement. It feels strange to be putting words to paper, so to speak. But at the same time, it's completely natural. I've already written two chapters, and they flowed very freely. Of course, I'm my own worst critic."

"I can't wait to read it," Gwen replied. "I love to read. Of course, I've had no time lately. But I'm hoping with a few more hires, I'll be able to get some semblance of a life back."

"I'm glad to hear that," Debbie replied. "Because Caleb and I were talking, and he suggested the three of us should do some travelling together. But I thought you might not be able to, with your schedule at the inn."

Gwen clapped her hands together. "Yes! I'm all for it. Of course, it might be a little while until I can manage it, but I want to travel. I've longed to travel for years. I was waiting for Duncan to retire so we could go together, but now that's a wash. So yes, sign me up."

"Me too," Joanna added. "I couldn't travel for so long, and even now the thought of it makes my stomach churn, but I'm dying to see more of the world. I feel as though I've hardly scratched the surface. There are so many interesting places to go, people to meet and food to eat."

"I'm happy to hear you're both interested. I'll start putting together some ideas of what we could do."

"That sounds wonderful," Joanna replied. "I can always count on the two of you to keep life interesting."

Chapter Twenty-Four

"Your social media accounts have really grown over the past few weeks," Beth said as she clicked through the inn's latest marketing campaigns on her laptop.

Gwen bustled around the kitchen, making breakfast. She poured hot water over a tea bag. "I'm glad to hear it. I love the branding you've done for the inn and restaurant, and I really think it's resonating with people. We've had a lot of new business thanks to you!"

"Oh, wow. An email just came through." Beth bit down on her lip as she opened the email. It was from a company she'd interviewed with a week earlier.

"Who is it from?" Gwen sat across from her at the small dining table with a bowl of cereal and a cup of tea.

"Manchurian Consulting."

"Oh, that job sounded like a good one. What do they say?"

"They're going to call me in a few minutes." Nerves erupted in her stomach as her phone buzzed. She picked it up. "Hello, this is Beth Prince."

The human resources manager responded and explained

that they would like to offer her the job of digital branding consultant. Beth happily accepted the position and hung up the phone.

"I got the job!" she said with a smile of glee.

Gwen grinned. "That's great news. I knew you would. You're so perfect for it."

"I think so too. It should be good. It sounds like there's a lot of flexibility, so maybe I can visit you more often. I've really loved staying here. I'm going to be sad to leave."

Gwen's smile faded. "Yes, I suppose you have to go. But where will you live?"

"Somewhere in Brisbane. I don't want to go back to the same area. Too many memories. I want to start fresh."

"You could try South Brisbane. It's lovely there."

"That's a good idea. I don't have to move until the new year, but that's not far off, so I should start looking."

"You don't have anything else on today, do you?" Gwen took a bite of cereal.

Beth shook her head. "I was going to spend some time with Jemma. I haven't seen much of her in years, and we kind of drifted apart. But with me back on the island, we've had a lot of fun together. It's like old times."

"I'm so glad you two are still friends. You were always like two peas in a pod."

"We were. She gets me in a way no one else ever has."

"Aside from your mother, of course."

Beth laughed. "Yes, other than you."

"We've had a good time this summer. Haven't we?"

"I've loved it. It's been so great to be back on the island full time. Honestly, if I didn't have to leave, I wouldn't."

"You'd get bored after a while. You're young. You should be off having adventures, meeting people, conquering mountains and that kind of thing."

"I'm not so young anymore. You were raising babies at my age." Beth replied.

"That's true. I think of you as young, but I guess you're right—I was in the thick of things at your age. Married, with children. It was a busy time."

"You weren't off having adventures, that's for sure."

"No," Gwen agreed. "Raising children was my biggest adventure. Still, I hope I get to have more adventures. I'm not done yet."

Beth offered a wry smile and patted her arm. "You will, Mum. This inn is definitely one of those—it's a huge project to take on, and you've done it so well. I'm really proud of you."

"Thanks, honey."

"You know what I should do today? I should go shopping."

"Shopping?" Gwen asked as she rinsed out her empty cereal bowl. "Don't you have to look for a flat in Brisbane? You need somewhere to live."

"I'll get around to it. But I'm going out with Jemma, and I need to finalise my Christmas shopping and get new clothes for the new job."

"Really?" Gwen shook her head. "I think you have plenty of clothes."

Beth laughed. "You can never have too many outfits."

"What do you think of this?" Jemma held a crop top up to herself and eyed her reflection in the mirror.

"I think it would look cute on you." Beth wore a pair of charcoal slacks and a matching suit jacket cinched tight at the waist by a narrow pink belt. She turned from side to side to view the outfit from various angles.

"That suit is perfect. You look amazing." Jemma pressed her hands together. "You have to buy it."

"It's expensive," Beth complained with a groan. "But I love it."

"It'll be worth it. And besides, you have a swanky new job. You can afford it."

"That's true. I'll be getting a substantial raise. And it's not like I have a family to feed." Her throat ached at the thought—what if it never happened?

"Your time will come," Jemma replied as she set the coat hanger on the hook in her changing cubicle.

"Will it?"

"Of course it will. You're still young."

Beth groaned. "I don't know about that. You have Dan. The two of you are happily married. No doubt you'll be having kids soon. And here I am, still all alone. No one to spend my nights with. No one to build a family with. And every time I think I've found him, he turns out to be..."

"A selfish jerk," Jemma finished the sentence for her.

"I didn't want to say it."

"But it's true, and if you can't say it, I will. He wasted your time and didn't think it was a big deal to break up over the phone. He was a jerk. Forget about him."

"The thing is, I knew I wasn't in love with him. But I thought maybe we could make it work anyway. Am I really so desperate?"

Jemma frowned. "You shouldn't settle. Even if you haven't found the one yet, don't settle. Marriage is hard. Trust me on that. You don't want to be married to someone you don't love."

"Is everything okay between you and Dan?"

Jemma sighed. "It will be. I'm sure it'll all work out. But we're fighting a lot at the moment. We're trying for a baby..."

"I'm so happy for you."

Jemma's gaze met hers. "We've been trying for two years."

"Oh, I'm sorry, hon."

"Yeah, it's been hard. And he's stressed at work. There's a lot going on. I'm only saying this to remind you that marriage is difficult. Look at your parents. They loved each other, and it still didn't work out. Don't tie yourself to someone you don't love. It's already difficult enough without adding that to the mix."

"You're right. I suppose I was just starting to think that maybe I've gotten it all wrong. That love is finding someone you enjoy being around and choosing to spend your life with them."

"You could do that, I suppose. But I don't think that would be enough for me. Or for you." Jemma picked up a pair of jeans and took them off the hanger. "You need a big love. Look at the way you were when you met Damien. You couldn't stop thinking about him for months. He was all you could talk about. It was sickening. I want you to find someone you can be sickening over. Just like that."

"I don't think I can still behave like a thirteen-year-old girl with a crush. I'm nearly twenty-eight years old."

"I'm sure you won't write his name on your binder. But you should have that kind of passion, and that compulsion to spend every moment you can with him."

"I want that," Beth agreed. "I want to find someone I can't bear to be away from."

"Yes! That's it," Jemma replied. "I have that with Dan. When we're not fighting tooth and nail, of course."

Beth laughed. "Oh, honey, I'm sorry. That sounds difficult."

"It is, but we'll be okay. Now, what do you think about these jeans for New Year's Eve?"

"I think you'll be far too hot in those."

"You're probably right, but aren't they cute?"

"Very cute. I'm going to wear shorts and a blouse," Beth said. "I was going to wear a sundress, but what if it's windy? Besides, I might like to go on some of the rides."

"I saw some really lovely shorts over here. They look like you could dress them up or down, and you could even pair them with heels."

"That's perfect," Beth replied as she followed Jemma out of the change room to find them.

"I need a dress for Christmas Day," Jemma said. "We're going to church with Dan's parents, and their church is kind of dressy."

"Something red?"

"Maybe, but it doesn't have to be."

"I'm glad you're coming to the New Year's festival with me."

"Dan wants to come with us. He said it'll be fun to see me in my element. He wishes he'd got to go to the festivals when he was a kid, since I've talked so much about them."

"He'll have a great time," Beth replied as she sorted through the shorts, looking for her size. She found it and held it up to the light. It was a dark blue-green colour, a little like the ocean. And she'd found a white sleeveless silk blouse that would go well with the shorts. "I like these."

"You'll look great in them."

Beth smiled. "Am I crazy for doing this?"

"Not at all," Jemma replied. "You're an optimist. And I love that about you. Besides, maybe he'll show."

"I doubt he's even given me one second's thought since that night," Beth said, her stomach forming a knot. But there was something deep down inside of her that was excited at the prospect of maybe, just maybe, seeing him again. And that excitement buzzed in her gut as she hurried to try on the shorts.

Chapter Twenty-Five

It was the day before Christmas and Gwen was at Joanna's for their Christmas-themed potluck brunch.

"I hope you don't mind, Joanna, but I've invited Fran today. It's kind of last minute, so I apologise for that." Gwen set a sweet potato casserole down on the bench beside the other dishes.

Joanna wiped her hands on her apron. "That's perfectly fine. We always have more than enough food to go around."

"Merry Christmas, all! I made prawns," Debbie said as she walked into the kitchen with a grocery bag, which she set on the bench beside Gwen's casserole dish. "And they're still warm, since I didn't have far to travel."

Gwen and Joanna kissed her on the cheek in greeting, and she took her dish out of the bag. Beth waved hello as she disappeared into Eva's room to see the baby. "Caleb is right behind me with the punch."

"Wonderful."

Caleb carried a large punch dispenser through the front door and set it on the bench with a grunt. "That's heavy. If you want me to move it, I'll do that now. Don't try to lift it yourself."

"Merry Christmas!" Joanna said as she embraced Caleb.

"Merry Christmas to you as well."

"One more day—I can't believe it's so soon. I'm not ready for it," Joanna replied as she spooned crispy potatoes into a bowl. "Christmas has snuck up on us this year."

"Is Emily coming today?" Debbie asked.

"No, but she'll be here tomorrow with her sister's family."

"That's nice. I hope you have a wonderful day together," Debbie replied.

"What will you do tomorrow?" Joanna asked Debbie.

"We're leaving this evening for a cruise."

"That sounds lovely," Gwen said.

"Yes, we're looking forward to it," Caleb replied.

There was a knock at the door, and Joanna opened it.

"Merry Christmas!" she cried.

Fran stood there with a bottle of red wine in one hand. "Merry Christmas," she said in a tentative voice.

Gwen bustled over to greet her. "Come on in, Fran. Everyone, this is Fran. Fran, these are my friends—Joanna, Debbie and Caleb. Oh, and here's Chris, too."

Chris walked through the door behind Fran and waved.

Fran nodded at each person. "Pleasure to meet you. Thank you for inviting me today."

"You're very welcome. Come on in and make yourself at home."

"I brought wine. I wasn't sure what else to contribute, since Gwen told me not to bring anything. I hope that's okay."

"It's more than okay. It's perfect," Joanna said with a wide smile as she took the bottle. "In fact, let's open it now and pour some for everyone."

While Joanna poured the wine, the rest of the group meandered into the dining room to find seats. The table had been set with green and gold china, crystal glasses and gleaming silverware. There were Christmas decorations sparkling throughout the room—a tall nutcracker by the door in his military suit, there were several regal gold deer scattered about, and stars hanging from the ceiling. Gwen had brought the decorations the day before on her way to the inn. She'd been run off her feet preparing for their first Christmas season and couldn't wait to collapse into a chair in exhaustion.

She sat with a sigh, wishing she could kick off her shoes. Instead, she took the offered glass of red wine from Joanna and sipped it. It was delicious and dry, just the way she liked it, and immediately a trickle of warmth sifted through her body.

The table was piled high with food. There was a honey-baked ham. Roasted turkey with stuffing. Crispy potatoes. Golden dinner rolls. Carrots and beans, along with a roasted pumpkin and couscous salad. Gravy to cover it all, and plenty of wine. It was a Christmas feast that Gwen couldn't wait to dig into.

Eva and Beth joined them, chattering and laughing together. Gwen was glad to see the two of them getting along so well, even though they were more than a decade apart in age. They were the youngest members of the group today, and Beth had been excited to spend some time with little Gypsy.

"Is the baby sleeping?" Joanna asked.

Eva gave a nod as she sat. "I've got a couple of hours—at least, I hope I do. She's been a bit unsettled lately."

"Never mind," Gwen replied. "Even if she wakes, there are plenty of hands ready to cuddle her today."

Eva flashed her a grateful smile. Gwen wondered how she was managing. She seemed to be coping well, but Gwen knew how challenging a baby could be, and Eva was only seventeen years old. She'd celebrated her birthday a few months earlier, and Gwen had helped decorate for the party. She was glad to see a few other local teenagers around Eva's age in attendance.

It was good that the girl was making friends. But she supposed that meant she was more likely to stick around, and Gwen wasn't entirely sure that being away from her parents at this difficult time was for the best. She wouldn't have wanted that for her teenaged daughter. But then again, she would've been supportive if Beth had fallen pregnant and chosen to keep the baby. How heartbreaking it must've been for Eva not to get that support.

Aaron, Emily and Wanda joined them in the dining room.

"I've seated the kids around the little blue table in the kitchen," Wanda said. "So they'll be running in and out, and I'll have to check on them. But so far, they're enjoying their meal."

"I'm so glad you could come. Take a seat, we're about to dig in," Joanna replied.

All three of them sat at the table. It was very full, with extra chairs added wherever they would fit. Aaron and Emily were practically in each other's laps, although Gwen doubted they would mind.

"Fran, how are you enjoying your time in Sunshine?" Joanna asked as she served Fran some turkey.

Fran smiled gently. "I love it here. It feels like home already."

"Where are you from originally?" Debbie asked. "I think Gwen told me, but I seem to have forgotten."

"I'm from Italy. Near Milan, specifically. My family was involved in the fashion industry there. They still are, but my husband and I trained in hospitality. So, when he got a job in Dubai, we went there to live. And my career followed his, so to speak."

"What an exciting life," Joanna replied.

Debbie piled plates with potatoes and handed them around the table. "Gwen tells me you've lived in some exciting places." Debbie said.

"Yes, I have. I like to go back whenever I can to see family. Of course, my husband wasn't keen on my travelling without him, and for many years, he worked a lot. Once he retired, it became a little easier, he didn't like to spend money on things he thought of as frivolous."

Gwen hid her reaction behind a napkin. Fran's husband sounded like a difficult man to live with. She had an intimate knowledge of just what that was like, and her heart went out to Fran.

"I'm happy to give you leave at any time to go and visit family. You just let me know," she said.

Fran met her gaze. "Thank you. I will do that."

"Do you have other family?" Caleb asked. "Brothers or sisters?"

"No, my parents have passed. They left me their entire estate, since I was an only child."

"Estate? That sounds like a lot," Joanna said. "Oh, excuse me, that was rude. I don't intend to pry."

Fran smiled. "It's okay. I don't know for certain how much it involved, since Marco took care of our finances, and he didn't think it was necessary...but the lawyer is putting together the final report..." She cleared her throat, her cheeks pink. "Excuse me. It is a difficult subject for me. I wasn't able to see my parents for several years before their passing."

"I'm so sorry," Joanna replied, one hand pressed to her heart. "That must've been so hard for you."

"It was. They didn't get along well with Marco. I wish I could've gone to see them more often."

Gwen felt anger rising up her spine. If Marco was still alive, she would like to have had a word with him. How dare he keep his wife from her family, and from any knowledge of her own financial situation. But there was no point saying anything about it now. He was gone, and any criticism would only hurt Fran.

"Well, I suppose you could see for yourself what your finances look like now that he's gone."

Gwen quietly filled her plate with food, her heart troubled. She was glad Fran had come into her life, and hoped that she would be able to help her new friend find her way back to happiness.

Chapter Twenty-Six

Christmas Day dawned bright and early. The sun rose at four thirty in the morning, carried on the wings of raucous birdsong. The heat was not far behind it. Joanna turned the air-conditioning on early, since she wanted her guests to be comfortable throughout the day. Most of the food had already been prepared. Joanna was exhausted, since she'd hosted the potluck brunch yesterday and was now hosting Christmas. But everyone had agreed to bring a dish, a potluck Christmas lunch, and it looked like a delicious spread so far. Eva had baked a chocolate cheesecake for dessert to be served with cream and fresh raspberries. Aaron and Emily had brought the roast pork with crackling. Wanda and the kids brought fresh seafood and a salad.

The guests had begun to arrive at around ten am, and by that time, the house was gleaming and Joanna was ready to relax. She welcomed them all and stowed their various dishes in the fridge. Then she set out snacks and nibbles for everyone to enjoy throughout the morning around the swimming pool. She changed into a swimsuit, along with her guests, and they all spent the next two hours splashing in the pool.

Emily made mimosas, and Joanna climbed out of the pool to sip hers while settled on a banana lounge. She watched as the two small children, wearing floats on their arms, squealed and laughed, leaping into the pool from the side and wearing their mother out.

Wanda soon joined Joanna for a mimosa while Emily and Aaron took over entertaining the children. Wanda didn't seem to have as much energy as usual, and Joanna worried that the cancer treatments were taking their toll. It made sense. She'd heard they could be brutal. And this was the second time Wanda had undertaken radiation treatments in the past two years.

"I'm enjoying your cookbook," Wanda said between sips.

"Thank you so much," Joanna replied. She adjusted her sunglasses.

"Especially, the potluck one. I love that you all got to contribute. It makes it even more special."

"It was so much fun. I think everyone enjoyed pulling it together and testing out all of the recipes," Joanna replied. "And how are you faring with your treatments? I hope you don't mind me asking."

Wanda smiled slowly. "I don't mind. They've told me that I'm responding well to the radiation. So, that's a good thing. I feel okay. I'm tired, a bit achy, but otherwise good."

"I hope it isn't all too much for you."

"Some days..." Wanda replied with a sigh. "The kids are a handful. But I'm grateful for Emily. She helps me more often than she really should. I know she's busy with school, but she's such a wonderful sister. I don't know what I'd do without her."

"Yes, she is. And a good friend. I'm glad she's there for you. But please don't hesitate to call if there's ever anything I can do."

"I think you have your hands full with Eva and the baby, not to mention the potlucks and your writing."

Joanna chuckled. "You're right about that. Still, I'm here if you need me. And I don't mind one bit."

"Thank you, Jo. I appreciate that."

After their swim, everyone showered and changed. Then they sat around the enormous Christmas tree that Joanna had paid to have install in her lounge room. She'd purchased it from a Christmas tree farm, but when it arrived, she quickly realised she wouldn't be able to manage it on her own. Thankfully, the driver was more than happy to assist.

It was a delightful forest green, and she'd decorated with red and gold, along with the eclectic collection of ornaments she'd gathered over the years to commemorate special events in her life, like the birth of a child or the sale of a book to her publisher for the first time. The ornaments reminded her of so many memories from the past. They had become an homage to her life, and one she treasured putting together each year.

Emily and Aaron sat close together on the love seat. He gave her a gold bracelet, and she gave him a leather jacket.

"You shouldn't have done that," he admonished her with a shy smile. "It's too much. And you can't afford it."

"I saved up," she replied. "You're worth it."

He kissed her then, and everyone watched with smiles on their faces. Joanna loved to see the two of them together. They reminded her of times long since past, when she and Ron had been very much in love and on the way to getting married. It'd been a happy time for her, and one she was very glad to see her grandson, Aaron, enjoying now with Emily, who was a dear friend.

At that moment, she missed Chris and wished he could've been there. He was visiting with his family, but he would be back in time to celebrate the New Year with her. Their recent conversations had given her hope that perhaps there was something more to their relationship than merely friendship. Maybe she was reading too much into things, or maybe he was simply taking his time, and that was fine with her. She had no desire to rush into something that could jeopardise their relationship if it went sour.

After the gifts were opened, they moved to the dining room. Joanna rushed about to warm everything and put it on the table, energy renewed after her swim and a few hours of relaxation. They gave thanks and dug in. The roast pork was moist, the potatoes crunchy, and everything was delicious. Joanna was grateful for all the help she'd received since she didn't think she'd have been able to pull it off alone, given everything else going on in her life.

Gypsy woke from her nap in time to join them and sat in her high chair, tossing pieces of food about the room with gusto and slapping the tray with an open palm as she shouted things like "Mumma!" "More!" and "Nanananan." Joanna loved that, since she was "Nan," and it'd been one of Gypsy's first words.

After the meal was over, Joanna was clearing plates when she heard a tentative knock at the front door. She went to answer it and found a young man with hair past his shoulders standing on the step, about to walk away.

"Can I help you?" she asked.

He spun back to face her, his cheeks pink. "I didn't think anyone would answer. I could hear the noise..."

"Sorry about that. We didn't hear you."

"It's okay. Is Eva home?"

"And you are?" Joanna asked, her eyes narrowing.

He shoved his hands deep into the pockets of some loose-fitting, low-hanging pants. His T-shirt was oversized, and his brown eyes darted from her face to the ground and back again. "I'm..."

Behind her, Eva gasped. Joanna stepped back to look at her. "Storm!" Eva shouted.

He shrugged. Eva rushed away down the hall to her bedroom. Joanna pursed her lips. "You'd better come in, then."

Storm followed her inside. The dining room was still loud, with everyone chatting and laughing over the remnants of their meal. No one else noticed what was happening. Joanna waved a hand at the kitchen table. "You can take a seat, if you like. I'll go and find Eva."

Joanna strode down the hallway to Eva's bedroom and opened the door. Eva was pacing back and forth, her thin arms crossed around Gypsy's body in a desperate hug. She looked up at Joanna with wild eyes, her face pale. "He can't be here. What's he doing here?"

Joanna went to the bed, sat down and patted the space beside her with one hand. "I don't know. I haven't had a chance to ask him yet. But I'm assuming he's here to see you and the baby."

Eva sat, puffing lightly. "I don't want to see him. He hasn't even bothered to come and visit Gypsy. It's like we don't exist. And he doesn't care. He doesn't care." She repeated the last phrase like a mantra.

Joanna rested a hand on her arm. "He's here now, honey. And he wants to see you. Let's worry about the rest of it when the time comes."

Eva let out a puff of breath. "Okay. I guess I can try that. But he doesn't deserve to know her."

"She deserves to know him, honey. He's her dad."

Eva's eyes filled with tears. She stood to her feet and crossed the room, then with a backwards glance at Joanna, she went out to meet the boy who'd broken her heart.

Chapter Twenty-Seven

Every year at Christmas, Debbie and Caleb had a tradition—
they went on a trip. It helped them through the years when
everyone else was having and raising children. They'd felt very
much alone at the time, since everyone they knew was
spending the day with family. They weren't close with their
parents, and so chose instead to spend that time with each
other.

In recent years, they'd stopped taking trips over the holidays, since they were barely speaking to one another. Instead,
they'd spent the day at home, quietly and separately. But now
that their marriage had been revitalised, Debbie was keen to
get back to having fun at Christmas, so she'd booked them on
a week-long cruise around the Whitsunday Islands.

It was only the first day, but so far, they'd had a blast
getting to know the other childless couples and families who'd
chosen to get away on a cruise ship over the holiday season.
The entire ship was decked out with Christmas decorations.
There were carols playing over the sound system, and there
was more food than either of them could possibly manage to
eat. She missed her friends and the beach house more than

she'd thought she would, but she was having a lovely time. She and Caleb hadn't gotten along so well in years. They were both relaxed and happy.

Christmas lunch was over, and they were both seated in recliners by one of the swimming pools. Debbie wore an oversized black hat, large sunglasses and a black bikini. Caleb had a book open over his face and was fast asleep. They'd both eaten too much and were feeling bloated and sleepy, but in a good way. There were several other couples at their table who they'd befriended over the past few hours, and they'd all drunk a little too much wine and had a lot of fun.

Debbie's head was still spinning. She thought she might take a dip, since the sun was boring down on them and making her hot. She applied some more suncream, and then stood to her feet. Her head felt light. She wobbled a little, then padded across the deck to the pool and climbed in. The water was cool. It felt good. She swam a few laps across the pool and back, doing a casual breaststroke. Children were playing and laughing, splashing and jumping into the water. Several couples lounged by the pool. Others joined in the fun with the children. It was nice to be around other people on Christmas Day, rather than at home just the two of them.

"Merry Christmas," a lady called to her.

Debbie waved. "Merry Christmas to you."

Everyone was jolly and friendly, and there was a show on that night with live performances by some acrobats and a singer who sounded incredible. She was looking forward to it. But she might head back to the cabin to take a shower and a nap first, since she suddenly felt extremely tired.

She climbed up the stairs and out of the pool. The deck was wet and slick. She felt herself lose traction before she realised what was happening, and suddenly she was flat on her back staring up at the blue sky overhead.

Pain radiated down her left leg. Her back ached. Her head hurt. She saw stars before her eyes and grimaced from the pain.

"Are you okay?" Caleb's face emerged in front of her, concern etched across his handsome features.

She groaned. "I don't know."

"What happened? I heard a loud bang."

"That was just my backside hitting the ground," she said between clenched teeth. "I think I've really hurt myself."

"Do you want me to get the paramedics?"

She raised her head from the ground. "No, I don't think so. I'll be okay. Help me up?"

He reached out both hands, and she did the same. Then he pulled her gently to her feet. She felt okay. Bruised and aching, but it didn't seem as though anything was broken.

"Is your head all right?"

She nodded, noting that the pain didn't increase. "It seems to be. There's probably going to be a lump on the back of it, though."

"Maybe we should get you checked out."

"Okay, that's fine. Let's go and then I want to head back to the cabin for a shower and a sleep. I'm feeling tired."

She took a step, then stopped. "Ouch."

"What hurts?" he asked.

"My back. It twinged." She squeezed her eyes shut as pain shot through her lower back again.

"Uh-oh. I hope you haven't done any real damage." Caleb put a hand under her elbow. "Can you walk?"

"I'll try."

She managed it, but they had to move slowly, with Caleb supporting part of her weight. He helped her to the first aid station, where they checked to make sure she hadn't injured herself too badly. It seemed a nerve was being pinched in her lower back and she was bruised all over, but otherwise she was fine. Her head injury was superficial.

Caleb helped her back to their cabin and into the shower. She could hardly move by the time she crawled into bed. He fetched the cream he'd brought with him for his bum knee from the bathroom, and rubbed it carefully and tenderly over her back, massaging the muscles with his fingertips as he went.

"That feels amazing," she said as he worked at a knot in her lower back.

"I've had almost an entire hour of massage training during a team-building activity at work," he said with a smirk in his voice.

She laughed, which made her wince in pain again. "Almost an hour? Wow, you're a professional. No wonder it feels so good." She hesitated, his words sinking in. "You massaged each other for a team builder?"

He chuckled. "No, we had a masseuse come in and show us some tips. We didn't touch each other—don't worry. I don't need lawsuits from the likes of you."

She grinned. "I would've come after you for that."

"I know you would," he quipped. "I've got your voice in my head, twenty-four seven, warning me what not to do."

"The perks of living with a lawyer," she replied, her voice soft as his efforts lulled her towards sleep.

"There are just so many, it's hard to keep count." He laughed and bent down to kiss the back of her head. "I'm going to watch the cricket. Enjoy."

As he sat on the couch and flicked on the television, Debbie could see him out of the corner of her eye. She couldn't help marvelling at how lucky she'd been to find him at such a young age, and to spend her life with a man she still loved so much. They couldn't have been a better match if they'd planned it out on paper.

Chapter Twenty-Eight

Kimmy raced past with a super soaker. She sprayed Beth, who squealed and crouched behind a hedge. Nolan was giggling uncontrollably on the trampoline as he shot his super soaker in every direction. The two younger kids were digging in the middle of the yard in a mud puddle they'd created throughout the water fight.

Beth tiptoed back to the house and slipped in the back door, leaving her muddy shoes behind. She found her mother seated in the living room, watching the bedlam through the back windows. Brandon's house was a roomy four-bedroom brick structure with a decent-sized backyard. It was sweltering hot, in typical Christmas Day fashion, and there was no swimming pool, so the entire family had taken to throwing water balloons and shooting each other out of enormous water guns after Christmas lunch.

The children were having a blast, but the tension between some of the adults was palpable. It was the first Christmas spent together with both her mother and father, along with his new fiancée. And even though there'd been no direct conflict so far, Beth had seen the way Mum had reacted to her father's arrival—her voice had taken on a higher pitch, and she'd avoided eye contact ever since. Currently, her father was outside doing his best not to participate in the water fight while talking Brandon's ear off. And his fiancée, Samantha, was in the kitchen chattering away to Brandon's wife, Mara, who had the patience of a saint, in Beth's opinion.

Beth was staying out of the way. She loved her father but felt sorry for her mother. It must've been hard seeing the young Brazilian woman on her ex-husband's arm at a family gathering, she didn't show it—not openly, anyway. But Beth knew her well enough to realise that her mother was uncomfortable.

"You coping?" she asked as she sat down next to Mum.

Mum had a cup of coffee in her hands. She was cradling it and looking out over the top of it as though she were hiding. "I'm okay. It's been a lovely day."

"You're doing well, Mum. I'm proud of you."

Mum glanced at her with a wry smile. "Thank you, honey. It's awkward, but I'll get used to it."

"It's not fair," Beth replied.

Mum shrugged. "Nothing in life is."

Just then, Nolan ambushed Kimmy, who consequently slapped him across the cheek. Nolan burst into tears and pointed a finger at her, shouting, "She hit me!"

Brandon intervened, and the low murmur of his voice, admonishing one and comforting the other, drifted through the glass that separated Beth from them. Her father watched the whole interaction from a distance with a look of irritation on his face. Beth knew it well. Dad didn't like loud, raucous behaviour. She'd seen that look a lot when she was young, it was usually followed by him yelling and sending someone to their room so they would miss out on the rest of the fun. He'd never had patience for them back then. She got on better with him now.

"Your father is a difficult man to live with. His new fiancée will have her hands full," Mum mused quietly before taking a sip of coffee.

"Why did you marry him in the first place?" Beth asked. She crossed her legs on the wicker couch, tucking her feet up beneath them.

"We were young. He wasn't so angry then. In fact, I don't think I ever saw him lose his temper. Not until we got married. Something for you to remember—men don't become who they're going to be until about twenty-five. If you marry them before then, it's like opening a Kinder Surprise. You never know what you're going to get."

"Really?" Beth asked.

"Really."

"I guess I'm safe, then, since I'm already past that age."

"It's a good time to get married."

"I don't know," Beth said. She chewed on her lower lip. "I'm not sure I'll ever get there."

"What do you mean?" Mum turned to face Beth, her attention fully fixed now on her daughter.

Beth leaned back with a sigh. "Mum, I'm twenty-seven, almost twenty-eight. My long-term boyfriend just broke up with me. It was two years between my last relationships. How long until I find someone new? Most of the good men are married."

"That's not true," Mum replied. "There are still plenty of good single men your age. People are getting married later and later these days."

"Yes, but they're already in those relationships, even if they haven't tied the knot yet."

"Do you think?"

"I don't know for sure, but it certainly seems that way."

"I suppose you could be right about that," Mum replied, returning her focus to the bedlam outside. "But I don't want

157

you to give up yet. You've still got plenty of time to find the love of your life."

"The love of my life? Is that even possible? I'm not sure anymore."

"Of course it's possible." Mum spun to face her, eyes wide. "Don't think that way. You're a beautiful young woman with your whole life ahead of you. There's a lot of love coming your way. You're just going over a bit of a speed bump right now. It happens to everyone at some point. You're getting yours out of the way now."

Beth laughed. "I hope you're right. But is it even worth it? Look at you and Dad... you loved him, put everything into your marriage. You gave up your career, your free time, your hobbies, everything for this family. And what did it get you? He ran off with a younger version the first chance he got."

"Maybe not the first chance. I can't say for sure how long he was cheating, and he refuses to answer that question."

"But was it worth it?" Beth really wanted to know what her mother had to say because inside, she felt all out of whack.

Mum reached out a hand to take hers and squeezed it. "I got you and your brothers out of the deal. So I win."

Beth rolled her eyes. "You have to say that. I'm your daughter."

"No, I don't *have* to say it. And it's true. You and your brothers are the very best thing I've ever done in my life. I don't regret marrying your father, even with the way things turned out, because we were happy for a long time, and we raised the four of you. Absolutely worth every single sacrifice, every pain, every tear to have you all in my life. And I know I gave you a hard time about taking me for granted last year, but the truth is, I was feeling low about your father. Our relationship had taken a turn for the worst, and I felt insecure. All of you have really tried to be better—to appreciate me and let me know it. And I've noticed. It's made all the difference in the world. So, thank you."

Beth smiled through a vale of tears. "Would you do it again?"

"What? Live my life over? Or be a wife and mother?"

"All of it."

Mum grinned. "I'd happily go through every single moment again if it meant I got to have you in my life. You're the very best of me."

As Mum got up to refill her coffee cup, Beth hugged her knees to her chest with a sob. It was good to hear Mum say the words. *It was worth it*. Every bit of pain she was going through and had been through, and would experience, was worth it for what she hoped one day to have—someone to love, and a family to raise with that someone. She couldn't give up on the hope yet. It would leave her hollow and empty if she did. She held on to it with white-knuckled resolve.

Chapter Twenty-Nine

Gwen's staff had managed to keep everything running for three days without her, and she was feeling rather chuffed over the accomplishment. This meant that one day, she might be able to take a longer vacation, something she'd hoped would be the case eventually. It felt good to have a few days off. She was refreshed and ready to get back into it.

Fran seemed quieter than usual. She was working hard and she had a pinched quality about her face. Everything seemed fine. But Gwen was concerned about her. Fran stood behind the reservations desk, working through the guest list, while Gwen tidied the entryway. She put a book back on a small floating shelf, then turned to face Fran, hands together.

"Your visitor the other day seemed a little emotional," Gwen said.

Fran met her gaze and gave a nod. "He was."

"Did he say why?"

Another nod. This was going to be more difficult than she'd thought. Fran wasn't one to share information she wanted to keep to herself. Gwen respected her privacy, but she was worried that Fran was facing something alone that would have a detrimental impact on her. What if she was in danger, and Gwen had done nothing about it? She admitted that was probably unlikely, but the point was, she didn't know. And she felt it was time she found out.

"What is his surname?"

Fran hesitated, her eyes dark. "Laccona. He's from my hometown of Bergamo. Near Milan."

"Oh? You grew up together?"

She offered a tight smile. "That's right. We were childhood friends."

"I thought you grew up in Milan."

"We spent a lot of time there and moved into the city when I was a teenager. My parents had a clothing company, and Milan is the centre of the fashion world. So, we travelled back and forth. They wanted us to be raised in a smaller town, and it's where my family is from originally."

"That sounds nice," Gwen replied, trying to imagine what it must've been like for Fran.

"It was a lovely place to grow. But I left it behind... for various reasons."

She wasn't going to give Gwen any more than that, and Gwen had work to do. But as she went to her office and set about paying vendors and suppliers, Fran's situation lingered in the back of her mind. She hated that Fran was in Australia alone since her husband's death. And now that a childhood friend had shown up out of the blue, Fran acted as though she wanted nothing to do with him. It was a very strange situation.

When she'd finished paying the bills, she did a quick internet search on *Bergamo*. What she discovered was a beautiful town with stone buildings in warm tones and cobblestone streets. Nestled amongst hills with snow-capped mountains as its backdrop, Bergamo looked like something from a fairy tale. How lucky for Fran to have spent her childhood somewhere so idyllic.

On a whim, she searched for *Alberto Laccona - Bergamo*. Search results filtered onto the screen—pictures of the man she'd seen speaking with Fran. Although most of the images were of a much younger version, in them he wore a suit and tie and often had a bank of microphones surrounding him. There were newspaper articles in Italian. Gwen didn't know any Italian, but she could recognise his name. She used a translator to understand one of the headlines. The recent headline read:

Mayor's Sudden Retirement Takes Bergamo By Surprise

Another, from ten years earlier, stated:

Mayor Alberto Laccona Set To Divorce Wife Of Thirty Years

Alberto was the mayor of Bergamo? Scrolling through the articles, it looked as though he'd been the mayor there for many years. There were photographs of him with a full head of black, wavy hair. Current images had his hair streaked with grey, the way he'd looked when he visited the inn. In the photographs he always wore a suit and tie, when Gwen had seen him, he was wearing a pair of slacks and a collared T-shirt. He still looked very fashionable and elegant. And now it made sense—he was a well-known politician. He must've given up on the fashion industry at some point and moved into politics.

He'd told Fran that he loved her and always had. Gwen had overheard their conversation. And Fran had pushed him away, told him she had nothing to give him. But there must be more to it than that, some kind of reason... Gwen was curious to know their history and what had caused him to come all this way. Were they in love once, long ago? Or was it a one-sided affair? What had happened to tear them apart? She had so many questions.

On a whim, she decided to run a search on Fran's name. Francesca Silver. She didn't expect to find anything much. From what little she knew of Fran, it didn't seem as though the woman had any social media accounts. She wasn't even sure Fran had a smartphone. She'd never seen her with one, but she had a phone number, so it must've been stashed in a pocket or purse somewhere. And there might not have been any reason for her to be featured in news articles over the years.

Gwen was surprised to see a number of articles fill the search results page. All the articles were in Italian, so once again, she decided to use a translator for the headline. What she read made her gasp.

Prominent Businessman's Daughter Missing

Gwen perused the article for a date. It looked as though it had been scanned in, since the article was blurred and in small-sized font. It was difficult to read, but there was a photograph. The image could've been a young Fran, it was hard to say. The date was largely illegible, it seemed to be from around forty years earlier, if she had to take a guess.

She quickly translated some of the article.

Francesca Barone has been reported missing by her family. She was last seen by her mother on Friday evening at six pm. Her parents say she was engaged to be married to well-known entrepreneur Alberto Laccona and would have no reason to leave of her own will. But friends of the young woman aren't convinced. They tell of a strained relationship with her family and that she often spoke of freedom.

Gwen stared at the words, her heart thudding against her ribcage. Was this really the Fran she knew? She had a different surname, but of course she wasn't married then. And the search results had returned this other name for a reason. If it was her, why had Fran run away? Or was she taken? Clearly, she'd survived the ordeal, whatever it had been. And now her long-lost fiancé had come in search of her. It was very romantic. Or maybe it was worrying. She couldn't say, since she knew none of the details. But she was intrigued.

Chapter Thirty

Joanna stared at the words on the page of the latest thriller she'd received as a Christmas gift, but she couldn't take in the story. She kept re-reading the same paragraph over and over again. The problem was, she could hear her granddaughter's phone conversation, and it was distracting her from the story-line. She couldn't concentrate on the book when all she wanted to do was eavesdrop. She probably shouldn't listen in, but Eva was speaking with her parents, and they were discussing her schooling. A topic in which Joanna was particularly interested. She was very keen for her granddaughter to finish high school. Having a baby at sixteen years of age shouldn't mean the end of her education.

So far, Eva had enrolled in a distance education program that was meant to begin the new term in a few weeks' time. But what if Eva changed her mind? Or Karen decided to contest her decision? Joanna strained her ears to see if she could hear the details of their discussion more clearly, but Eva was in her bedroom and Joanna was in the living room. Just then, Eva walked out to the kitchen and opened the fridge to stare at its contents. It was a ritual she completed several times per day.

"I'm looking forward to it, Mum. Don't worry," Eva said with an exasperated sigh. "I'm going to do my best."

There was silence for a few moments, then, "I know I failed a few tests the last time I was at school, but I also had a lot on my mind. I want to finish school so I can get a job. I've got to support Gypsy at some point. And Storm says he's going to get an apprenticeship so he can work and send us money too."

Joanna was glad to hear that. Eva hadn't shared the details of Storm's visit. The two teens had simply disappeared on a walk down to the beach with the baby in her pram. They'd been gone for hours, and when Eva came back, she and the baby were alone. She wasn't open to discussion, either, and had simply grunted in response to the few questions Joanna asked her.

Just then, her own phone rang, and she was forced to give up her eavesdropping to answer it. She felt like a guilty child, caught out doing the wrong thing.

"Hello?"

"Hi, Jo. It's Chris."

She smiled. She'd missed him over Christmas and couldn't wait to see him again. The sound of his voice sent a buzz of excitement up her spine.

"Hi, how are you? Did you have a nice Christmas?"

"It was lovely. The kids were over the moon about all the gifts they received. They really are spoiled to death. It's a bit much, actually, but we had a great time. And it's been so nice to spend uninterrupted time with them. I wish you could've been here."

"I wish I could've been there as well." She couldn't wipe the grin from her face. "Will you be home soon?"

"Not long now."

He wouldn't give her a specific time, and she couldn't understand why. She was dying to see him and had planned to cook a special meal for his first night back at home.

"If you send me your flight details, I can pick you up from the airport," she replied.

"No need," he said. "I'll just take an Uber."

"Oh, that's so impersonal."

"It's fine. Don't worry yourself over it," he said with a laugh. "You always want to help, and I'm so grateful for it. But I don't like to overtax you. You've got to look after yourself as well, and I know you've been working hard over the Christmas break with all your guests and parties."

She sighed. "You're right. I'm feeling a little wiped out—I will admit that."

"I was calling to ask if you're free for New Year's Eve."

"I'm free," she replied. "Why do you ask?"

"I thought I might take you on a date."

"I'd love that. Where will we go?"

"How about the Sunshine Beach festival? I go every year, and it's one of my favourite traditions. I thought we could share it together this time."

"I haven't attended in such a long time," she replied. "I'm excited to go. It will be even more special with you."

"I'm glad to hear it. Also, I've left something for you at the front door."

"My front door?" she asked, glancing in that direction. "When? How? What is it?"

"It's a surprise. Why don't you go and take a look? I'll wait."

She hurried to the door. She couldn't imagine what he'd left there. And when did he do it? If it was before he went away, she would've seen it before now. Maybe he'd had something delivered, but she hadn't heard anyone pull into the driveway.

"What have you done?" she asked as she pulled the door open to search the front porch.

Chris stood there with the phone pressed to his ear. He grinned. "G'day."

He pushed his phone into his pocket and held out his arms with a grin.

She cried out in delight and rushed to embrace him. His arms went around her, she pressed her cheek to his chest. Her heart hammered, she felt breathless. It'd been so long since she'd felt safe in the arms of the man she cared about. In that moment, she realised how strong her true feelings were. He'd been by her side through some of the most difficult seasons of her life. He'd encouraged her through the worst of her illness and recovery. He'd always had a kind word to share and had never judged her. He was truly the best person she knew.

She looked up at him with tears in her eyes. "I can't believe you're here. You should've told me you were coming. I would've made you something to eat or picked you up..."

He laughed and brushed her hair back from her face. "I didn't want you to go to all that trouble. I want to be the one who spoils you sometimes."

It was then that she saw the bunch of red roses in his left hand. He gave them to her. She held them tight, studying the beauty of their intricate petals, inhaling the fresh, fragrant perfume.

"They're lovely. Thank you."

Then he leaned forward and pressed his lips to hers. It took her breath away. Her eyes drifted shut as his lips explored hers. Warmth flooded through her body, and she raised her hands to encircle his neck, still clutching the flowers. Then on tiptoe, she reached up to deepen the kiss. His arms wrapped around her waist, pulling her closer until her body was pressed up against his.

Chapter Thirty-One

It was New Year's Eve, and Debbie was feeling a bit down. She wanted to go to the festival with her friends, but she'd injured her back on the cruise and still wasn't feeling up to doing much. So, she and Caleb had decided to stay home and celebrate alone. It felt as though the Christmas season had bled into New Year's and they were still on their own—something she wasn't accustomed to, they'd had a great time on the cruise despite her injury, and she loved being with Caleb. She hated to miss out on the New Year's Eve fun, and so instead of mooning about it all day, she'd spent the past few hours working on her book. It'd taken her mind off the festival and given her a way to focus on something constructive.

While she worked, Caleb went grocery shopping, leaving the house quiet. Her back ached, the pain had lessened since they returned. She'd seen their physiotherapist several times since Christmas and had gotten a massage the day before. The massage only seemed to make things worse and she'd hardly gotten a wink of sleep the previous night. When it seized up, she felt as though she might cry out in pain. But the spasms were less frequent today, and she was starting to believe she might recover within a week or two if things kept going the way they were.

After a while, she heard Caleb's car in the garage. She eased herself to her feet with a grimace and hobbled out to meet him.

She met him in the kitchen. "Hey, honey. Any more bags to bring in?"

He set two bags of groceries on the bench. "No, this is it. And I wouldn't let you carry them anyway. You've got to take it easy if you want to get well. You know what the physio said."

She peered into one of the bags. "I know. But it's hard to sit around and not do anything."

He kissed the tip of her nose. "It's hard, is it? Sounds like an idyllic life to me."

She laughed. "You know what I mean."

"I know you can't stand not being able to do things for yourself. But maybe it's time you let someone else take care of you for a little while and relax."

She groaned. "More relaxing? I feel like that's all I've been doing lately."

"You're really struggling to get into this whole retirement thing, aren't you?" He began unpacking the groceries onto the bench. "You're going to have to learn how to take it easy, since this will be the rest of our lives. Besides, don't you feel like slowing down? I know I do."

"It's true. I don't have the energy I used to have. But I've always gotten my value from achieving..." Even as she said the words, she knew how bad they sounded.

He sighed. "You don't need to achieve to be valuable to me. I love you and appreciate you just the way you are."

"Thank you." She loved that he felt that way about her. But she still found it difficult to accept. Who was she if she wasn't achieving? Wasn't contributing something to the world?

Caleb returned to the garage.

"I thought you said that was all of it," she called after him.

He didn't respond, so she sorted through the groceries. There were two large steaks, some potatoes, corn on the cob, snow peas and a frozen cheesecake. He loved those frozen cheesecakes and always snuck one into the shopping trolley whenever he went to the grocery store.

There was a packet of crackers, as well as a wheel of camembert. She opened them both and sliced a piece of camembert onto a cracker. She slid it into her mouth and chewed with her eyes shut. Delicious.

Caleb came into the kitchen behind her and set a box on the bench.

"What did you get? Wine?" she asked.

He shrugged, a self-satisfied smile playing around the corners of his mouth.

Her eyes narrowed. "What is this? What are you smiling about?" He was up to something, that much was clear. But she couldn't figure what it was.

She opened the top of the box and looked inside. A tiny white kitten with a black nose, ears and paws mewed up at her.

She startled, then stepped back. "What? A kitten?"

He laughed. "Go on, pick it up. It's a Ragdoll."

"A Ragdoll?" What did he mean by that? It looked like a cat to her.

"That's the breed. They're supposed to be really sweet."

"Oh." She reached into the box, and her hands closed around the kitten. Its fur was so soft, it was like cuddling a cotton ball. And it was so light, she lifted it into the air easily.

"It's a he, by the way," Caleb said. "So you'll have to come up with a masculine name."

"A boy? Oh, he's so cute. I can't believe you got me a kitten. I've never been a cat person. Or a pet person, for that matter."

He shrugged, slicing himself a piece of camembert. "I thought it was time we became cat people. Why not?"

She held the kitten up to her face. Its blue eyes were half-hooded, and it mewed softly. It was adorable. There was no questioning that. But could she take care of a cat?

With it held against her body, she went out to the back patio and sat in a rocking chair. She rocked it gently, and it fell to sleep within a few minutes. A little ball of fluff between her hands.

"I suppose this means you can't help with dinner," Caleb quipped, his head poked out between the back sliding doors.

"I don't want to disturb him. He's probably stressed about the move to a new location, away from his mother. And he's sleeping."

Caleb grinned. "You just relax. I've got it covered anyway." He brought a tray out with the steaks, potatoes cut into chips, and the corn, then got to work at the BBQ grill.

While he cooked, they discussed the kitten. Where he should sleep. How they would train him. What they would do with him when they travelled. Finally, they discussed what they should name him.

"How about Finn?"

"Finn?" Caleb asked. "Why not something more... cat-like?"

"What, like Patches?"

"Yeah."

She huffed. "I don't know. That's so clichéd."

"Okay, name him whatever you like."

"How about Camembert?"

He laughed. "Really? You're going to shout *Camembert* when it's time for him to come inside?"

"We could shorten it to Cam. It's what I was eating when I met him."

"Okay, Camembert it is. I prefer Cam though."

When he woke, he had a lot more energy and playfully swatted at anything that moved. They ate together and laughed over the kitten's antics. Caleb had bought him bowls for food and water, along with a collar and some kitten food. So, after dinner, Debbie filled his bowls and set up a blanket for him to sleep on. She'd go to the pet store the next day to get everything else he might need. She was already feeling very attached to the small creature. She'd been surprised by her emotional connection. It was something she hadn't experienced before and wasn't expecting.

It wasn't long before Cam wanted another sleep. Debbie picked him up again and cradled him in the rocking chair. The early fireworks at Sunshine Beach lit up the recently darkened sky. She quickly covered Cam's ears to keep him from being frightened, and he slept through the whole thing. The fireworks were a dazzling display of golds, yellows, reds and greens. They were very loud, since Caleb and Debbie's beach house was so close to the shoreline. But she appreciated being a part of the celebration.

Those fireworks were for the families with children. There would be an even larger display when midnight rolled around, and soon it would be a whole new year. A year without work, or her business. Without much of anything to occupy her time. But now she had a kitten, was writing a book, and it felt as though she finally had something to look forward to.

Chapter Thirty-Two

Beth Prince stared at her reflection in the mirror. Wide blue eyes stared back at her. Her face was pale, apart from a few freckles that stood out on her nose. She was nervous. Too nervous. It was silly. There was very little chance that a boy she'd met at thirteen would be waiting for her at the festival fifteen years later.

Her birthday the day before had been uneventful. She'd turned twenty-eight and celebrated by going to the movies with her mother. It wasn't exactly the type of outing she'd grown accustomed to in her twenties, but it'd felt right. Nothing was the same as it had been, and lately she'd become more appreciative of her family and wanted to spend time with them. Nightclubs were a thing of the past. She no longer felt any desire to dance the night away with a bunch of strangers as she had a few years earlier.

These days, she preferred the simple pleasures of life, and she'd had a wonderful time watching a romcom with her mother, eating at the *chocolaterie* next door to it, and reminiscing about her childhood. They'd laughed and cried over various anecdotes, and then shared secrets they'd never told one another before. It'd left Beth feeling more bonded to her mother than she'd ever been. It was a precious memory she'd treasure forever.

"Are you ready to go?" Jemma finished tying her hair into a knot.

"I'm ready." Beth took one last look. She'd left her hair down. It fell in blonde waves over her shoulders. It'd grown much longer in recent months and had been bleached lighter by the days spent in the sunshine and swimming at the beach. Her skin was tanned from the sun, and she was fitter than she'd been in years. Life in Sunshine had brought back her youthful glow, something she'd lost by so many years of living in the city, commuting to a high rise in order to spend her days sitting in front of a computer. She felt good.

Jemma pressed hands to each of Beth's arms and looked her in the eye. "Dan's still at work, so he's meeting us there later. But just a reminder that no matter what happens tonight, we're going to have fun. This is a New Year's Eve to remember. Who knows where you'll be this time next year? And maybe I'll have a baby. We might not get to do this again. So, let's just enjoy it for what it is. Okay?"

Beth gave a nod. "Yes, you're right. Of course we're going to have a great time. No matter what..." If he showed. If he didn't show. It didn't matter. This was a special evening. She and Jemma were celebrating their tradition of attending the festival together. They hadn't done it since high school, and who knew if they ever would again. She had to remind herself to be present, to take it in. Life was flying by too quickly, and she wanted to slow it down.

They walked from the flat to Sunshine Beach together. The sun was still up, but it was sliding down the western sky, leaving trails of pink across the deep blue. The ocean was calm with small, gentle waves curling to shore. Already there were hundreds of people on the beach, and more parking and walking from the various side streets around it.

There was a parkland beside the beach, and carnival rides, food stands and more set up on the grass. The beach was full of people playing volleyball and beach cricket, or laying on towels to soak up the last of the sun's rays.

"What should we do first?" Jemma asked when they arrived.

"I haven't eaten a thing all day," Beth said. "I've been so nervous. Let's get something."

"What do you feel like?"

"Dagwood dogs are my favourite."

They lined up at one of the food trucks and ordered Dagwood dogs. A hot dog on a stick, covered in breading. It was topped with tomato sauce. They sat on the grass overlooking the beach and ate. It was delicious, and brought back so many good memories for Beth.

They spent the next two hours walking on the beach, riding the Ferris wheel, playing darts and drinking lemonade. Finally, they lined up to buy churros with chocolate dipping sauce. The entire time, Beth had scanned the crowd, looking for Damien. She hadn't seen him. But she'd spotted plenty of other people she knew and had stopped to talk with at least two dozen so far —former high school classmates, former friends, and boyfriends as well as family members. It seemed almost the entirety of Sunshine's residents as well as many out-of-towners were there.

Beth spied Joanna and Chris seated on folding chairs with Emily and Aaron. They were all eating hamburgers and chattering together so loudly that Joanna almost didn't see Beth. She waved at her, and Joanna finally waved back. She came over, wiping sauce from her face with a napkin.

"Hi there, Beth. Are you having a nice time? Hello, Jemma."

"Hi, Mrs Gilston," Jemma replied.

"We're enjoying it so far," Beth continued scanning the crowd.

"Looking for someone?" Joanna asked.

Beth sighed. "Not really. I thought someone might be here... but he's not. I don't know why I expected him to show. Did Mum tell you about my thirteen-year-old crush?"

"Oh yes, that's right, we've heard all about him," Joanna replied, patting her arm. "Don't worry about all of that. Just have fun. It's a beautiful night. And those hamburgers are to die for, if you're hungry."

"We have churros coming," Beth replied.

"Ooooh, churros. I know what I want for dessert," Joanna said.

She returned to sit with her friends, and Beth sighed. "I know I shouldn't have had my expectations up, but I can't help it."

Just then, she spotted a man. There was something about him that caught her eye. His back was to her. He was watching the Ferris wheel turn. Then he spun slowly around, studying the crowd with his brow furrowed.

Her breath hitched. It couldn't be him. She hadn't seen him in fifteen years. And even then, she'd only known him for one night. There were no photographs to go by, since she hadn't owned a phone. And she didn't know his surname, so she'd never been able to search the internet for pictures of him.

But it could've been him. He looked familiar. He was taller now. Broader shoulders, too. His brown hair flopped around a wide cowlick in gentle waves. His golden-brown eyes were wide and kind-looking. His handsome face was more chiselled than she recalled. And he was much more muscular. He wore a V-necked T-shirt and a pair of shorts. His skin was tanned. And he was clearly searching for someone.

Chapter Thirty-Three

The busy evening shift was over, and it was time to relax. Most of the guests at the inn had gone down to the festival. There was a packed restaurant, but Gwen wasn't needed. She'd done all she had to do, and since it was New Year's Eve, she'd decided to finish her night on the back deck with a drink. She mixed herself a cocktail, a lemon drop martini, and sat with her legs propped up on a chair. The entire deck was empty, so she had the place to herself.

She wasn't alone for long, though, since Fran soon came outside. She sighed and pressed both hands to her face, unaware at first that Gwen was there. Gwen cleared her throat. Fran looked up in surprise.

"Oh, sorry, Gwen. I didn't realise you were here. I'll leave you alone."

"No, please don't. If you'd like, I've mixed up some lemon drop martinis, and you're welcome to join me. We can celebrate the New Year together."

"You're not going down to the festival?" Fran walked closer and pulled a chair over to sit with her.

"Not this year. I'm tired, and I don't think I could spend an evening on my feet after the day I've had."

"I totally understand," Fran said, collapsing into her chair. "I feel the same way."

Gwen went to the bar to pour Fran a drink, then carried it back to her. They clinked glasses.

"Cheers," Gwen said.

"Cheers," Fran replied. She sipped. "Oh, this is good."

"Thanks. I make a pretty mean lemon drop. I love a nice sour drink."

"I'm used to drinking only wine. But this might be my new favourite."

"What kind of wine do you enjoy?"

"My family has a vineyard. We make our own chianti."

Gwen frowned. "Really? Wow, that's special."

"I miss it. I miss them."

"I'm sure you do. How long has it been since you were there?"

"A long time. And I've grown accustomed to being away from them now."

"What was it in particular about your hometown that your husband didn't like?" Gwen asked, as she sipped her drink.

Fran swallowed and drew a deep breath. "It was Alberto."

* * *

Beth studied the man standing next to the Ferris wheel. His gaze flitted over her and kept going. Beside her, Jemma was quiet.

"Is that him?" Jemma asked in a small voice.

"I don't know. Maybe. It was so long ago."

"He's searching the crowd. It could be him. I can't believe this." Jemma's incredulity echoed her own.

"It couldn't be him," Beth said as if by rote.

"There's only one way to find out."

Beth glanced at Jemma, who dipped her head in his direction, then gave a quick nod.

Beth's gaze returned to the man, who looked as though he was about to walk away. She'd have to move quickly. She broke into a jog, then slowed her pace as she neared him. Her heart hammered in her chest. She felt as though she couldn't breathe. Her head was light. Was this really happening? If it wasn't him, she couldn't allow herself to be devastated. The chances were slim. It wasn't a big deal. She tried to convince herself.

"Excuse me," she said in a soft tone. Her voice was carried away on the ocean breeze. She cleared her throat and tried again. "Excuse me." This time she spoke louder, and the man's attention turned to her, his golden-brown eyes focused on hers.

"Hi," he said. He smiled, and dimples lit up each cheek. Dimples just like the ones Damien had.

"Is your name Damien?" Straight to the point. It was a simple, direct approach, but the only one that really mattered in that moment. She needed to know. Only he had the answer. She could feel Jemma hovering in the background, watching.

His eyes widened. "Beth?"

A lump rose in her throat. It was him. He was here. After all these years. He'd come back.

"Yes, I'm Beth." She didn't know what else to say. What do you say to the boy you'd secretly loved since you were thirteen, and who was now a full-grown man? A very attractive and slightly intimidating-looking man? She swallowed around the lump in her throat, willing it to go away. She didn't want to sound like an emotional mess. He'd think she was a crazy person.

He grinned wider. "I didn't think you'd come…"

"I can't believe you're here," she replied at the same time.

They both broke into soft laughter.

"Would you like to take a walk on the beach?"

"I'd love that," she replied.

She fell into step beside him. She glanced at Jemma. Dan was with her. She waved a goodbye and mouthed *good luck*. Beth smiled in response.

"How far did you travel?" Damien asked.

"I live here. So, I walked for about five minutes."

"That was convenient."

"How about you?" she asked.

"I flew here from Sydney. I still live in Dee Why. I work there now as an engineer. I've got my own firm—well, I share it with my dad and my brother."

"Did you have some work in Brisbane?"

He shook his head. "No, I came to see you."

She gaped. "I didn't think you'd remember."

"I've thought about you a lot over the years. The connection we had... it was special. I've never found one like it again. Of course, I've told myself over and over that we were so young, it's not likely to be the same now. But I had to find out. You know what I mean?"

"I know exactly," she replied. "I feel the same way."

They walked along the beach. At some point, his hand found hers. They fit together perfectly. It felt good, right. Their conversation was natural. Later she wouldn't remember what they spoke about, but recalled that there was a lot of laughter. The chemistry was there. The spark she remembered from before.

"Why did we choose fifteen years as our catch-up?" he asked.

"We thought that was about the time we'd be wanting to get married. And maybe we'd like to marry each other." Her cheeks burned.

184

He laughed. "Oh, yeah, that's right. Perfect timing."

"You're single?" He was holding her hand, so she hoped he was. But she had to know for certain.

"I broke up with my long-term girlfriend about six months ago. I've been single ever since. You?"

"I've been single for a little over two months."

"As I said, perfect timing." He squeezed her hand.

They stopped there, sat in the sand, and chatted for hours. At midnight, the sky was lit up by a brilliant display of fireworks. It was so close to them, they both had to cover their ears to keep from being deafened. The fireworks shot high above the water, leaving reflections that were as spectacular as the show itself. Beth huddled close to Damien against the cool of the late-night breeze that blew in from the ocean. He wrapped an arm around her shoulders, and she leaned into his side. Everything about the night seemed as though it couldn't possibly be real. She looked up at his profile as he watched the display. She couldn't believe he was there. It was something she'd dreamed about for fifteen years, and now it was happening. She had never felt so happy.

Chapter Thirty-Four

Gwen took another swig of her martini. Her head was beginning to spin, since this was her second cocktail. She'd have to order an Uber or have one of the staff drive her home. But it was New Year's Eve, after all. Why not have a little celebration?

"What reason did Marco have for keeping you away from Alberto?" Gwen asked.

Fran's cheeks were pink in the soft glow issuing from the lighting dotted around the deck. "Alberto was my first love. We were going to get married. But then I met Marco. He was older, charming. He swept me off my feet. At first, anyway. I was so young and naïve, I didn't know what to think. And he was very forceful. He told me we would only talk, but without my knowledge he drove me away from there—away from my family and from Alberto. I was scared. I didn't want to go with him, but by then it was too late. I didn't have a way to get back home again. And so, I married him. I was afraid of him. I thought I had no choice."

Gwen hadn't expected that. She wasn't sure what to think. "Why did you stay with him so long?"

"I got pregnant. And then I knew I couldn't leave. Most of the time, he was a good husband. Took care of me. Taught me about the hospitality business. We had a life together. I tried to leave him a few times, but he had the children. So, I came back. Piece by piece, I died a little more inside until there was very little of me left."

Gwen rested a hand on Fran's arm. "I'm so sorry. I had no idea..."

"It's okay. I loved him in my way. He wanted to be a husband, a father, and he did the best he could. He loved me so much. But I have many regrets."

"What about your family? What did they say?"

"They gave up on me. At first, they were beside themselves and wanted me to come back. But when they learned we'd been married, they washed their hands of me. Said I was no longer their daughter. That I'd brought shame on the family and that I wasn't welcome there."

"Oh, that's awful." Gwen's heart ached for her. She couldn't imagine saying something like that to one of her own children. "Alberto has come here looking you after all these years, hoping for another chance. Why did you turn him away?"

Fran sighed. "I'm afraid."

"Afraid of what?"

"That it won't be... as good as it was. He won't love me when he gets to know me as I am now. That my family will be angry with me. My husband hasn't been gone long..."

Gwen shook her head. "Your family will understand. You gave so much of your life to Marco. If you don't feel that way about Alberto, you should let him know that."

Fran's eyes glistened. "But I do. When I see him, my stomach churns. In a good way. Do you know what I mean?"

Gwen smiled. "I know exactly what you mean. If that's how you feel about him, you should talk to him about it."

"You think I should give in to love?"

Gwen laughed at her sweet way with words. "Absolutely I do. If you care about him and he cares about you, why wouldn't you dive in head first? That kind of spark doesn't come along often."

"Perhaps you are right."

"At our age, we can't live in fear any longer," Gwen continued. "What does it matter what anyone else thinks? Live your life. Love if you can. I hope one day I'll find the same kind of passion that has brought Alberto across the world to see you again."

Fran inhaled a quick breath. "I'm too old..."

"Nonsense!" Gwen replied. "You're never too old to love."

Fran gave a quick nod. "You're right. I've lived in fear for far too long..."

Just then, someone burst through the back door and stormed onto the deck.

"Francesca!" a man's voice called out.

Gwen stood to her feet, startled. "Hello Alberto."

He smiled at her and nodded. "I'm so sorry to intrude, but I'm looking for... oh, there she is. Francesca, we need to talk."

Gwen glanced at Fran, who nodded to her. Gwen walked away to give them some privacy, but didn't go too far in case Fran needed her. She sat on the other side of the deck, sipping the rest of her drink.

Alberto took Fran's hands in his, then kissed the back of each one. "I know you're still grieving that man who stole you from me. I wish you'd chosen me all those years ago, but I'm here to beg you to consider me now. I have nothing to give you but my heart. I hope it will be enough."

Gwen's throat tightened. His words sent tingles up her spine. How could Fran resist?

Fran sighed. She raised a hand to cup Alberto's cheek. "I didn't choose him all those years ago. He took me against my

189

will. I never told you that because I was ashamed. I let him do it. I let him convince me you didn't really love me, that my family was against me. I was young and stupid."

Alberto's voice quavered. "I wish he was here so that I could..."

Fran pressed a finger to his lips to quiet him. "There's no need to talk about him any longer. He is gone."

"Will you give me another chance now? Most of our life is gone, but we still have time to be together. And I will never rest comfortably if I don't try one last time to win you."

Fran offered him a wide smile. "It's always been you, Alberto."

Then he kissed her. It was passionate and intense. Alberto's arms were around Fran. Hers snaked around his neck. One leg was raised to entwine around his. Gwen stood to her feet and hurried inside, shutting the door quietly behind her. Her heart racing, she leaned against the door. Her eyes squeezed shut, and she groaned—oh, to have a love like that. She could barely imagine it. Duncan had never loved her that way. They'd been friends, had fun together, enjoyed each other's company, but never with that kind of passion. It was too late for her to experience that now, but she was grateful that Fran would have a second chance with her first love. And for now, that was enough.

* * *

After the early fireworks, Joanna and Chris had gone back to her place to play Scrabble. They'd played for hours, talking and laughing. They'd drunk a bottle of wine, and her head was feeling light. She'd served crostini with tomatoes and cucumber. Then ravioli with cheese sauce. And finally, a decadent chocolate mousse for dessert.

He finished his chocolate mousse with much spoon scraping. "I'm going to get fat if we eat like this too often."

She laughed. "No, we'll simply go for a walk on the beach tomorrow and have a light breakfast. It'll be fine. I eat like this all the time. It's about balance."

"Balance? I like the sound of that." He grinned at her. "I'm glad I have you to remind me of such an important life philosophy. I can get very single-minded."

"I'm happy to help," she replied as she took his empty bowl. "Would you like coffee? More wine?"

He patted his stomach. "I'm fine. And it's almost midnight. We should watch the fireworks."

She nodded. "Perfect. I'll just put this away and be right back."

She brought two small glasses of brandy with her, warming them with her hands as she walked. She handed one to Chris. "It's brandy. The perfect way to ring in the New Year."

"Thank you. Do you have any resolutions?" he asked.

She hesitated. "I don't usually make them. I think that's because I rarely kept them in the past, since anxiety caused me so many issues and made me procrastinate and feel overwhelmed by any goal, big or small. So, this year, I've decided to try one—I want to take more risks. It's not really something you can measure, so I'm probably getting it all wrong. But that's my resolve—to risk more."

"I think you're already doing well there," he replied.

"Thank you."

"You know, you've made such a difference in my life."

She blushed. "I'm glad. You've done the same for me. I was thinking about that recently—just how much you've added. You've always been so encouraging, and I truly appreciate that."

He smiled. "I'm glad. But it's easy to say nice things to you because you're such a wonderful person."

She laughed. "I'm not always so wonderful, or easy to deal with. But you're kind anyway, so thank you."

"I mean it," he replied seriously. "I don't always express it well. My deceased wife called me stoic. But perhaps that simply means that I'm not great at communicating my feelings because I don't feel stoic inside."

"What do you feel?" she asked.

He paused. "I care about you a great deal. You're the person I think about most. You're on my mind in the morning when I wake up, and when I go to bed at night."

She didn't know how to respond, but she loved hearing those words. "You're communicating well now."

He laughed. "I suppose I am. I'm trying, anyway. I don't want there to be any confusion. That's all."

"Consider things cleared up," she replied, taking his hand in hers. "And ditto."

Then he kissed her as fireworks exploded across the night sky.

Chapter Thirty-Five

The next day, Beth slept in. She'd stayed up late with Damien. They watched the sunrise on a new year, just as they had all those years ago. On the same beach. Watching the same sun rising over the same ocean. It was like déjà vu, and she loved every minute of it.

But now, at noon the next day as she padded into the kitchen with a gigantic yawn, she couldn't help wondering if it'd all been real or imagined. Mum stood in the kitchen in a pair of silk PJs, cooking at the stove.

"Good morning," Beth said.

"Afternoon, more like," Mum replied with a grin. "You got in late."

"So did you," Beth retorted. "You forget, I have a notification on my phone when there's movement at the front door."

"Touche."

"What did you get up to?" Beth sat at the kitchen table and pulled some grapes from the fruit bowl. She ate them one by one.

Mum scooped eggs onto two pieces of toast, then handed a plate to Beth.

"I spent some time with Fran. Then I came home. I wasn't sleepy, so I took the dog for a walk. There were still so many people out and about—I was surprised. What about you? Did Prince Charming appear?"

Beth grinned as her mother sat opposite her. She didn't speak until Mum looked at her with a curious frown.

"Really? You're joking, right?" Mum said, eyes wide.

Beth laughed. "No, I'm not joking. He was there. He came all the way from Sydney to see me."

"I can't believe it. I was sure you'd be disappointed today. I bought loads of chocolate home from the inn with me. Thought we could binge *Pride and Prejudice* and eat chocolate bars."

"Oh, you of little faith," Beth replied before taking a bite of scrambled eggs on toast. "Although I still want to do that, so pencil it in for later."

"So, now what?" Mum asked.

Beth shrugged. "I don't know. I'm a little worried he'll realise in the light of day just how much he'd exaggerated my appeal and will scurry back to Sydney without saying goodbye." Saying the words out loud made her throat hurt. But she laughed to soften the blow.

Mum's brow furrowed. "Beth! Don't say things like that. You're a beautiful, smart, fun and accomplished young woman. Any man would be blessed to have you in his life. And if he walks away now, that would be his mistake."

Beth sighed. "Thanks, Mum. Anyway, we're supposed to meet for dinner tonight. We're going to the Black Cat. I raved about their chicken and pumpkin salad. So, he suggested we eat there."

"That sounds good."

"Now I have to figure out what to wear." She hadn't

thought this far ahead. Her entire focus had been on the New Year's Eve outfit. She began to mentally run through the list of outfits she owned. There was a decided lack of attractive and classy clothing in her closet other than her work outfits.

"You should wear the white shorts with the black-and-white halter top," Mum said. "You look great in that ensemble."

Beth considered it. "Good idea. Thanks. You've got really good taste, Mum. You should've been a stylist."

"I try," Mum said as she popped a forkful of eggs into her mouth.

Just then, Beth's phone rang. She stood to answer it, then walked out of the room for privacy.

"Hello?"

"Hi. It's Damien."

She grinned. "Hi. Did you get any sleep?"

He laughed. "I've only just woken up. I'm still trying to open my eyes." And he'd already called her. That had to be a good sign. Unless he was calling to cancel.

"Me too," she replied. "I'm eating eggs with Mum."

"So, you've already had breakfast?"

"In progress."

"Can we meet for coffee? Unless you've got other things to do this morning..."

"Coffee? I'd love that. What time?"

"Is half an hour okay?"

"Perfect. Let's meet at Mum's restaurant. It's got the best coffee around, and that's not my bias speaking, I promise."

"Great. I'll pick you up in half an hour."

Beth hung up the phone and hurried back to the kitchen to finish her breakfast.

"Was that him?" Mum asked.

"It was." Beth sat down. "He wants to meet for coffee in half an hour. So, I've got to get in the shower. Fast."

"I guess this means he's not walking away," Mum said with a sly look.

"Not yet, anyway," Beth replied, feeling excited as she hurried to the bathroom to shower.

* * *

Damien picked her up as soon as she was dressed. She didn't have time to apply makeup, and her hair was still a little damp. But it would have to do. When he knocked on the door, she glanced at her reflection one last time with a sigh and hurried to grab her purse.

The Aurora restaurant was open for lunch, so Beth asked for a table outside on the deck. It was a beautiful day, even though it was sticky hot. She was thankful for the light breeze that blew in over the ocean and through the tables at the restaurant.

There was a good crowd gathered for lunch. Beth was proud of what her mother had achieved. Already the restaurant had the feel of a place that'd been around for a while. The locals enjoyed the food and the tourists raved about it, which meant that it was often fully booked. Beth was certain she was only given a table at the back of the deck because she was the owner's daughter.

They ordered coffees and a slice of cake each. And then Damien reached for her hand and held it while they talked. And they couldn't stop talking. They never ran out of topics of conversation. He was widely read, and they were able to discuss books. Then she spoke about travelling, and he'd already been to several countries that were on her list of places to go. He told her all about them and made her long to travel even more than she had before.

"I have to go back to Sydney tonight," he said suddenly.

She frowned. "Do you really?"

He laughed. "Yes, I do. I've got work tomorrow. I honestly didn't expect to find you, so I didn't think about staying longer."

"Can't you postpone?"

"I wish I could, but I'm working on this project... Why don't you come with me?"

"Come with you? I can't do that. You're leaving today."

"You don't have to travel today. But would you consider moving to Sydney? What are your plans?"

She startled. This was unexpected. "I've been offered a job in Brisbane. I was set to move back there in a few weeks. I just need to find a place."

"Since you haven't actually signed a lease yet..."

"I don't know... I've never lived there. I don't know my way around. Where would I go? What would I do? I have a job lined up in Brisbane."

He grinned. "I'll help you figure it out. But I really think we should see where this thing between us might go. All these years, I regretted not getting your contact details, not staying in touch. I don't want to live with those regrets again. And long distance won't work. We need to be close to one another and really give this a try. It's what I want. What do you want?"

She hesitated. She wanted that too. But it was scary—the idea of moving to another city where she didn't know anyone other than him. Changing her entire life for him. But if she didn't take the risk, she might always wonder what if.

"I'll think about it," she said. "I promise."

Chapter Thirty-Six

Later that day, Beth sat down at the kitchen table with her laptop. She couldn't stop thinking about what Damien had asked her—would she consider moving to another city for a man she barely knew? It seemed crazy. She didn't want to ask her family or friends about it because she knew how it sounded. Why would she give up a good job offer and the chance to be close to family and friends for a man she'd met one night fifteen years ago? It didn't make sense.

And yet, she wanted to do it. Every part of herself was excited at the prospect, even if that excitement was tinged with nerves. She drew a deep breath and started searching for jobs in Sydney. There were dozens of search results. She clicked on each of them and noted the requirements, the salary, the location. There were several in Dee Why. This was possible. She could get a job in Sydney doing what she loved and live close by to Damien. And if they dated and it didn't work out, she could move home again.

The prospect scared her. What if she wasted a few more years of her life on another man. But what if it lasted and they were meant to be together? She had to take the chance. There was something about him that lit her up inside. Something she'd held on to for fifteen years. All this time, he'd been in the back of her mind, the man she compared every other man to. The one she thought about when she felt nostalgic or missed home.

He'd always been there in her memory and imagination. But now he was very real. She had to take this chance. If she didn't, she'd regret it forever, and might never find someone she had this kind of chemistry with again.

She closed her laptop and went for a run along the beach. Then, after a shower, she dressed for dinner. She felt serene, but with a buzz of excitement down her spine.

He picked her up at six, then drove her in his rental car to the café. He'd booked them a table inside, in the air-conditioning, but with a view of the beach. The sun hadn't yet set, and there were people surfing, swimming, playing beach volleyball and basically enjoying the beautiful evening after a swelteringly hot day.

The café was a small, quaint place. It jutted out across the sand, with a series of outside tables on a weathered deck. The inside tables were covered in red-and-white checked tablecloths with a small candle at the centre of each. It was early, but several of the tables already held families. A baby sat in a high chair and sucked on a squeeze yoghurt. A toddler drove a toy car across the floorboards, his parents begging him to shush. And a young couple in love leaned over the table to whisper to one another.

Beth and Damien held hands across the table. His touch sent a jolt of joy through her and made her skin tingle. He was so handsome. His dimples made her smile. And the kindness in his voice was calming to her nerves.

"You okay?" he asked once they'd placed their order.

She nodded. "I'm just nervous."

"Me too," he replied. "But happy."

"Yeah, that as well. I was thinking about what you said."

"What's that?" he asked.

The waiter brought their wine, a bottle of Merlot, and poured it. Beth hesitated. This was an important conversation. She didn't want to be interrupted. She needed to get her thoughts out in a coherent way. When the waiter left, she took a sip of wine, then spoke again.

"You asked if I'd move to Sydney."

He dipped his head in assent. "That's right. I think we should be close to one another to see if it will work. I would move to Brisbane, but I'm part of a family business. And since you haven't started your new job yet, and haven't found a flat, I thought..."

"No, you're right. I'm mobile. I can move. There's no reason for me to stay here, other than the fact that this is my home. But home can be anywhere. And so, I'd like to try—I'll move to Sydney. If you still want me to."

He grinned and kissed the tips of her fingers. "I want you to very much. I can't wait to spend more time with you. And a long-distance relationship would be torture."

She laughed. "Then it's settled. I'll move down there. I can live close by, but I won't move in with you."

"I don't want us to move too fast either. Let's take things slowly and see how it feels. If we push it, we could destroy this thing we have between us, and I don't want to risk that. We'll date, and if we decide it's not going to work, we can part ways. I hate that you have to start a whole new life to make that happen, but I think it's the only way we can really give ourselves a genuine chance."

"Let's do it," she agreed.

He stood to his feet and pulled her up onto her toes, then wrapped his arms around her waist. He stared into her eyes, his own deep and darkened with passion. Then his lips found hers. He was tall, so she had to reach up to snake her arms around his neck. Her fingers wound through his hair, and she felt heat rush up her body and through her gut.

Someone nearby cleared their throat. The two of them pulled away from one another guiltily.

"We should probably wait until after dinner for that," he murmured.

Beth's cheeks burned as the others in the restaurant sent knowing looks their way.

She laughed. "Well, at least we know *that* part of the relationship won't be an issue."

He inhaled a sharp breath. "You can say that again. And now we can relax and get to know one another the old-fashioned way. I'm looking forward to every single moment with you."

She ducked her head, unused to the loving way he already spoke to her. But she could definitely grow used to it. There was something so gentle and encouraging in the way he expressed himself, and as she met his gaze, she couldn't help imagining their future together, all the years of love and friendship, the children they might have, and the adventures they'd go on together. She knew her life would never be the same again.

* * *

Thank you for reading **The Summer Pact***! I hope you enjoyed visiting Sunshine, Bribie Island. And if you'd like to visit with Joanna, Debbie, Gwen & Emily again, you can order the next book in the series,* **A Sunshine Christmas** *now.*
Return to Sunshine with Book 4...

"**Love, love, love** these books!"

Want to find out about all of my new releases? Click here to be notified about new stories when you download this free book!

Keep scrolling to find out about all of my other books.

If you'd like to join my Facebook reader group, where we talk about what we're reading and have other fun together, you can do that here.

Also by Lilly Mirren

ALSO BY LILLY MIRREN

It's been five years since Maree divorced Jack. They married too young and when things got tough, they found they couldn't keep it together. She remained in Sunshine and he moved away with his family. But now he's back and his presence in the small, beachside hamlet threatens to upend her carefully constructed single life.

CORAL ISLAND SERIES

The Island

After twenty five years of marriage and decades caring for her two children, on the evening of their vow renewal, her husband shocks her with the news that he's leaving her.

The Beach Cottage

Beatrice is speechless. It's something she never expected — a secret daughter. She and Aidan have only just renewed their romance, after decades apart, and he never mentioned a child. Did he know she existed?

The Blue Shoal Inn

Taya's inn is in trouble. Her father has built a fancy new resort in Blue Shoal and hired a handsome stranger to manage it. When the stranger offers to buy her inn and merge it with the resort, she wants to hate him but when he rescues a stray dog her feelings for him change.

Island Weddings

Charmaine moves to Coral Island and lands a job working at a local florist shop. It seems as though the entire island has caught wedding fever, with weddings planned every weekend. It's a good opportunity for her to get to know the locals, but what she doesn't expect is to be thrown into the middle of a family drama.

The Island Bookshop

Evie's book club friends are the people in the world she relies on most. But when one of the newer members finds herself confronted with her past, the rest of the club will do what they can to help, endangering the existence of the bookshop without realising it.

An Island Reunion

It's been thirty five years since the friends graduated from Coral Island State Primary School and the class is returning to the island to celebrate.

THE WARATAH INN SERIES

The Waratah Inn

Wrested back to Cabarita Beach by her grandmother's sudden death, Kate Summer discovers a mystery buried in the past that changes everything.

One Summer in Italy

Reeda leaves the Waratah Inn and returns to Sydney, her husband, and her thriving interior design business, only to find her marriage in tatters. She's lost sight of what she wants in life and can't recognise the person she's become.

The Summer Sisters

Set against the golden sands and crystal clear waters of Cabarita Beach three sisters inherit an inn and discover a mystery about their grandmother's past that changes everything they thought they knew about their family...

Christmas at The Waratah Inn

Liz Cranwell is divorced and alone at Christmas. When her friends convince her to holiday at The Waratah Inn, she's dreading her first Christmas on her own. Instead she discovers that strangers can be the balm to heal the wounds of a lonely heart in this heartwarming Christmas story.

EMERALD COVE SERIES

Cottage on Oceanview Lane

When a renowned book editor returns to her roots, she rediscovers her strength & her passion in this heartwarming novel.

Seaside Manor Bed & Breakfast

The Seaside Manor Bed and Breakfast has been an institution in Emerald Cove for as long as anyone can remember. But things are changing and Diana is nervous about what the future might hold for her and her husband, not to mention the historic business.

Bungalow on Pelican Way

Moving to the Cove gave Rebecca De Vries a place to hide from her abusive ex. Now that he's in jail, she can get back to living her life as a police officer in her adopted hometown working alongside her intractable but very attractive boss, Franklin.

Chalet on Cliffside Drive

At forty-four years of age, Ben Silver thought he'd never find love. When he moves to Emerald Cove, he does it to support his birth mother, Diana, after her husband's sudden death. But then he meets Vicky.

An Emerald Cove Christmas

The Flannigan family has been through a lot together. They've grown and changed over the years and now have a blended and extended family that doesn't always see eye to eye. But this Christmas they'll learn that love can overcome all of the pain and differences of the past in this inspiring Christmas tale.

MYSTERIES

White Picket Lies

Fighting the demons of her past Toni finds herself in the midst of a second marriage breakdown at forty seven years of age. She struggles to keep depression at bay while doing her best to raise a wayward teenaged son and uncover the identity of the killer.

In this small town investigation, it's only a matter of time until friends and neighbours turn on each other.

HISTORICAL FICTION (WRITING AS BRONWEN PRATLEY)

Beyond the Crushing Waves

An emotional standalone historical saga. Two children plucked from poverty & forcibly deported from the UK to Australia. Inspired by true events. An unforgettable tale of loss, love, redemption & new beginnings.

Under a Sunburnt Sky

Inspired by a true story. Jan Kostanski is a normal Catholic boy in Warsaw when the nazis invade. He's separated from his neighbours, a Jewish family who he considers kin, by the ghetto wall. Jan and his mother decide that they will do whatever it takes to save their Jewish friends from certain death. The unforgettable tale of an everyday family's fight against evil, and the unbreakable bonds of their love.

About the Author

Lilly Mirren is an Amazon top 20, Audible top 15 and *USA Today* Bestselling author who has sold over two million copies of her books worldwide. She lives in Brisbane, Australia with her husband and three children.

Her books combine heartwarming storylines with realistic characters readers see as friends.

Her debut series, *The Waratah Inn*, set in the delightful Cabarita Beach, hit the *USA Today* Bestseller list and since then, has touched the hearts of hundreds of thousands of readers across the globe.

Made in the USA
Middletown, DE
26 December 2024

68161903R00128